Radiant
DARKNESS

To Plainfield
Public Library —

Emily Whitman

Radiant
DARKNESS

EMILY WHITMAN

Greenwillow Books
An Imprint of HarperCollins*Publishers*

Radiant Darkness

www.harperteen.com

The text of this book is set in 11-point Galliard.

Book design by Paul Zakris

Library of Congress Cataloging-in-Publication Data

Whitman, Emily.

Radiant darkness / by Emily Whitman.

p. cm.

"Greenwillow Books."

Summary: Persephone runs off to the underworld with Hades, with whom she has fallen in love, but when her mother Demeter threatens to destroy the earth to save her, Persephone finds a way to come back once a year, bringing spring.

ISBN 978-0-06-172449-7 (trade bdg.) — ISBN 978-0-06-178035-6 (lib. bdg.)

[1. Mythology, Greek—Fiction. 2. Persephone (Greek deity)—Fiction. 3. Hades (Greek deity)—Fiction. 4. Demeter (Greek deity) —Fiction.] I. Title.

PZ7.R784Ra 2009   [Fic]—dc22   2008029148

09 10 11 12 13 LP/RRDB First Edition 10 9 8 7 6 5 4 3 2 1

Greenwillow Books

For Kate and Sam—
and for Richard:
His arm will be my home.

Prologue

"PERSEPHONE. *Daughter of* DEMETER, *the harvest goddess. Kidnapped and forced to—*"

Wrong! In every book of myths, the same; in every book, wrong!

Oh, I know it all got complicated because of the choices I made. I'm not trying to pretend I'm blameless.

Still, after thousands of years, I wish people knew what really happened when I walked in my mother's flowering vale and the black horses landed, crushing flowers and filling the air with heady perfume.

Just once I'd like to set the record straight.

PART ONE
Above

I hate eternity.

The Problem with Immortality

"Stay here, Persephone," says my mother. "I have some work to do."

As if I could go anywhere.

She's all dressed up in her goddess clothes—the chiton dyed purple with rare sea snails; the golden girdle embossed with waving wheat; the emeralds dripping like green leaves from her neck, her arms, her golden hair. She looks about twenty feet tall.

Off to rescue the world, probably. Mrs. Black-soil-springs-from-my-footsteps. Mrs. Even-the-grain-greets-me-with-lowered-head.

Is that what she wants me to do, bow down and worship her? That's for mortals, not me.

"I'll be back tomorrow afternoon," she says. "You'll be safe here in our beautiful vale."

Our vale? It's *hers*. This place has nothing to do with me. It's all about *her* flowers, *her* waters, *her* rich earth.

"While I'm gone, make sure you thread the loom. And watch your yarn choice this time." She reaches up and fingers the fabric near my shoulder. "Pale colors are so unattractive with your black hair."

She's always giving me advice.

It's not like it used to be when I was little. Back when she still smiled at me. When she didn't always pinch her mouth like she's trying to keep her temper trapped inside. I remember sitting by her knee, watching her nimble fingers turn fleece into long, silky threads. "Coax fine cloth from fresh wool," she used to say in her flowery way.

But these days her advice isn't about teaching me things. It's about tamping me down, squashing me into the right shape, like a potter slaps clay around until it's his idea of a beautiful vase.

I could take it for a day, or a week, or a month. But we're immortal.

Here's the problem with immortality. Every day is exactly the same. I'm stuck forever with my mother telling me to comb my hair, put my clothes away, stand up straight. I always sleep in the same bed. I always walk by the same olive trees down to the same lake, its pebbles worn smooth by an eternity of lapping water.

My mother bends to fix her sandal strap and catches sight of my legs. She comes up with a disapproving expression. "That dress is too revealing, dear. Go change."

"But—"

She doesn't wait to listen. Turning to leave, she calls over her shoulder, "And remember not to step on the thyme: it's blooming."

As if I hadn't noticed.

Why should she care if my dress is too revealing? She's created a world devoid of men. The only men I see are painted on vases. The only men I hear about are in the stories my friends tell.

I've spent my whole life here. I'm sick of it.

The Meadow

I wake to a new smell in the air, not the everyday over-ripeness of summer, but something bright and fresh, like the first spring bud bursting open. The scent is so strong, I look to see if my mother has placed a vase of flowers by my bed, but the top of my trunk holds only the usual bronze mirror and the same old red clay foxes, and the house is silent. Then I remember: my mother, leave me a gift? Not likely. She's gone to bless the fields. I decide to follow the scent and see what flower is calling to me with such a loud voice.

On the trail down to the lake, I stop and sniff, try-ing to decide which way to turn. The well-worn path is already toasty under my soles. Dust rises in the heat and the early-morning sun soaks into my skin as if it were midday. A tortoise plods along beside the path, one heavy foot in front of the next. He stops to nibble some rosemary leaves, releasing a burst of their sharp smell. A rustle behind me makes me turn. It's only a deer. She stares at me with huge, knowing eyes.

I can smell the leaves and flowers pulling in light from the sun, releasing their own perfume in return—roses, sage— the familiar smells of home trying to take over and distract me from their new rival. Then, suddenly, a faint branching appears in the trail. There, to my left, is a small path I've never noticed. As soon as I see it, the fresh scent grows stronger, winning the battle for my attention again, and I head up the slope in a new direction. Why have I never come this way before?

The dusty path gives way to soft grass under my feet. The trail is only the faintest line now, a whisper of deer hooves, as I walk into the shade of linden and poplar trees, and the deep green of olive leaves on gnarled branches. The perfume is stronger with every step, and I feel like I'm being reeled in on a string. My breath grows shorter and faster. It must be the steep trail making my heart beat so hard.

Now plum trees, thick with ripening fruit, block my view. I lift a heavy branch from the trail and the air lightens, as if a hand were lifting a veil from my eyes. A meadow spreads out before me, but I barely look at it—I only have eyes for the flower beckoning a few steps away. A gentle white head bobs on a slender stalk, sweet and unassuming, like a daffodil's little sister. But her perfume blares out so insistently, I almost feel drugged, like I'm in a different world. In a trance, I reach toward the stalk, and the wind blows my hair back.

Wind? There's no wind today.

I lift my head, and my mouth gapes open. Four gigantic black horses are treading air above the meadow, pushing great gusts with feathered wings. Their heads toss atop massive, muscular necks. Behind them, a golden chariot blazes in the morning sun. A hand holds the reins. A strong, wide hand. A man's hand.

Who is he? What is he doing here?

I freeze, except for my heart: it's crashing around in my chest loud enough for the whole world to hear. What if that man hears and sees me staring at him? A shiver of fear runs down my spine.

He must have pulled on his reins because the horses are landing, their mighty hooves touching down as lightly as a sigh, black wings folding gently over strong, broad backs.

I pull my eyes away and stare at the ground as if it could swallow me up and make me invisible: the long, heavy grasses; a small frog hiding under a leaf, its chest rising and falling almost as quickly as mine.

Suddenly, two birds burst into raucous song, shattering

my trance, and I remember I'm capable of moving. I edge back under the trees. Once I'm hidden again, I start running, quietly at first, then faster and faster, until I'm shoving branches out of my way and trampling right over poppies, scattering their blood-red petals across the path. A pounding, like drums, sounds an alarm in my ears.

When I reach the fork in the trail, I screech to a stop, panting and clutching my sides. And listening. But I don't hear anything, except my heart trying to break out of my ribs.

My mother is going to kill him! She's going to kill me!

But I ran, didn't I? Like she would tell me to. I barely glanced at him. So I must be imagining that bold, straight nose. The black beard framing strong cheeks. And those eyes. I'm probably making them up, those black eyes burning like coals in the hottest part of the fire.

The deer pokes her head out from behind a branch, then turns and ambles down the path as if nothing happened. I follow, but I'm seeing the texture rippling in his hair, the travel cloak draped over one bare shoulder, a hand pulling easily on the reins.

Maybe he came to visit my mother.

Ha! Seeing him must have addled my brain. My mother, welcome a man?

I lift my eyes from the trail. There's the lake, as blue and placid as ever. Ringing the lake are meadows stuffed with flowers and trees bowing heavy with fruit. And surrounding it all—I look up and there they are—cliffs, towering pink in the morning light. They're the prettiest prison walls you ever saw.

And my mother did it all for me.

When I was born, she always says, she still had festivals and harvests, and I would have been in her way. So she created this all-female sanctuary, calling to nymphs—flowers and trees, breezes and streams—and they came gladly, filling the vale with music and perfume. At first some of them were my nurses; now others are my friends.

Without any men around, my mother figures I'm safe and she can ignore me. She dons her harvest goddess clothes and heads off to her temples. Or she just wanders oblivious, drunk on germination, among grapevines and lemon trees.

I bet she thinks if I'm not around men, I'll never have to grow up.

I look down at my hands. I'm not voluptuous and golden like my mother, with her blue eyes and small, perfect features. I'm thin and strong. My hair is a wild black mane, and my mouth is, in my mother's disapproving words, "a bit too generous."

I shiver. Clouds are starting to cover the sun and the last trace of pink disappears from the cliffs. I could climb the highest tree in the vale and still not see over to the other side.

His tunic was banded in purple. Sea-snail purple. That means he's someone important. His skin was golden brown.

She'd know who he is.

I kick a pebble and it arcs downward, like the curve of my mother's lips. It buries itself in the bushes crowding the sides of the path.

As I round the last bend, I can feel the ground pulsing with my mother's green energy. She's back already. I look down the path and there she is, by the rosemary bush, stroking a leaf with that faraway look on her face. She's changed back into the white chiton she always wears at home, and she's barefoot, feeling the earth with her feet. She's taken off all her necklaces and bracelets so they're not in the way as she plucks a grape from the vine and pops it in her mouth. Even from here I can see her smile, wiggling her toes in the grass and lifting her face to the sky with her eyes closed. She turns her hands upward, like a plant soaking up sun.

And I know I can't tell her. She'd go all tight and tense. She'd make me start a weaving marathon. Shackle me to my loom. Sit by my side all day. Looking at me.

I don't need to know who he is.

Who he was.

He won't be back, anyway.

The Sacrifice

My wooden doll. I wove her scarlet dress myself when I first learned to spin wool and thread it on the loom. I was new to the shuttle's dance, so the fabric is rough.

My red clay foxes, small enough to fit in my hand.

My old spinning top.

I gather them all in a basket, carry it to my mother, and say, "I'm ready."

"Ready?" She pauses in her weaving, the shuttle frozen in midair.

"I'm ready to sacrifice my toys."

To take them to the temple, like mortal girls do. To lay them before Artemis and tell her I want to let them go. I can weave. I'm as tall as my mother. I'm ready to enter the world of women.

My mother's eyebrows look like they're yanked up by a rope. "I don't think that's necessary just yet." She pauses, then says in a soft voice, "Why, I remember when I brought those foxes home and how happy you were when you opened the box."

I think of all the mortal girls who have ever gone to that temple. I imagine them in one long line. Their hair is woven with ribbons and flowers. They're wearing bright chitons and unscuffed new sandals. Their baskets are heavy with clay dolls and wooden dolls and fabric dolls, with carved animals and old rattles. Their mothers walk proudly beside them. The parade heads up a hill toward towering columns.

My mother turns back to the loom and her hand resumes its rhythmic work, back and forth, back and forth. "Don't be in such a rush," she says. "Give yourself a little longer to enjoy being a child."

The other girls file past olive trees and lavender. I hear their breath, short and heavy, on the steep path.

"Mortals have to make their little sacrifices. You're the daughter of a goddess. You can keep your dolls." She smiles, as if this were a gift.

They pass through gleaming marble pillars into cool, dark shade. Now they're laying their armloads in front of the statue. The air hangs heavy with incense. Their mothers stand straighter.

"But, Mother—"

"Go ahead; put them back in your trunk. I don't think we need to talk about this again."

She's not looking at me anymore. I whirl around and rush back to my room.

I slam the door and hurl the basket. Everything goes flying. The doll lands on the bed, burying her face in the covers, and the top goes skittering across the floor. One of my red foxes crashes against the trunk and breaks into a million pieces.

I slump down and start to pick up the fragments one by one.

She's never going to let me grow up. Another thousand years will go by and I'll still be sitting here with my doll and my spinning top.

"Mortals have to make their little sacrifices," she says.

Well, if someone came to me with mortality in a box, I'd open it. Childhood and Adulthood would be sitting there, next to gray-haired Age, his beard trailing behind him. Grief would be shrouded in black, and Death would hold a knife by his side, ready to cut off each and every life at the stem. I'd see them all there and I'd still grab that box, because then I'd get to change.

She got to change, didn't she? Ripening into her god-nature, becoming the all-powerful goddess of the harvest.

Having me. Then, and only then, did she stop, as if her essence was set in stone. That's how it is for most of the gods: they grow into their full power and then stay that way for eternity, never aging, never lessening.

But what if *this* is as far as I get? Look at Eros, the boy-god of love: he's a child and always will be. What if that's my lot? Frozen on the cusp of life. Demeter's daughter and nothing more. For eternity.

I put the shards on top of the trunk and stare at the plants outside my window. I can almost see them stretching their roots into the soil and their stems up to the sun, getting ready to blossom and seed. I'm the only living thing in this whole damn vale that doesn't get to grow.

Gods! I can't believe how stupid I was. I had one chance to meet a man, and I ran away. Who was he? Why was he here?

I can't even ask my friends. They'd talk. My mother would find out and twine herself around me like ivy, so tight I couldn't move. I'd be trapped in this room forever.

The Latest about Zeus

My friend Kallirhoe lives in the stream near the linden tree. Moss carpets the broad stepping-stones in a patchwork of small stars and little furred trees. Water ripples around the rocks, bubbling with Kallirhoe's laughter. When she comes out, she's still part of the stream. Her arms trace curves like lines on water, and she walks like she's flowing over the ground.

Kallirhoe knows everything that's going on. All the nymphs and dryads sit by her stream, and she overhears what they're saying. I'd like to say she can't help it, but that's not true. She loves knowing secrets about broken hearts and longing glances.

But she also knows everything because she's so easy to

talk to. She looks so innocent, with those wide blue eyes and that little curved mouth. She asks all the right questions, and you feel like she really cares and understands. If you're not careful, all your secrets just pour out of you. The next thing you know, she's sitting around with everybody saying, "Did you hear? Did you hear?" And everyone's laughing and having a great time. I really think she can't help it. Talk flows around her like water, too. It's hard to keep water closed up.

I love Kallirhoe, but you won't catch me telling her anything personal. I don't need my life spread all over the vale. If someone else saw the golden chariot, let *her* say something.

Right now she's dipping her toes in the lake. We're all lying around on the shore. Our bodies are still wet from swimming, but the sun is drying us fast. "Did you hear the latest about Zeus?" she asks.

I run my fingers through my wet, tangled hair, easing the knots out, and try to pretend my heart isn't beating so fast. Could it have been Zeus in the chariot? After all, only an immortal would have winged horses. I smell the white flower again, as if it were right in front of me. I see the man's smoldering eyes, his black hair, the purple-banded tunic draped over one bare, brown shoulder.

Admete raises her eyebrows. She's a stream naiad, too, but a wild mountain stream, rambunctious and hard to keep in its banks. "Not again! What did he turn himself into this time? Another shower of gold, to show off his flaxen hair?"

Flaxen? So it wasn't Zeus after all.

Not that it matters. The chariot wasn't in the high meadow yesterday when I went back to gather plums, or when I strolled by this morning. He was only there once by mistake, I bet. He was passing over on a long journey and the horses needed to graze and he saw the field. That's all.

I turn my attention back to Kallirhoe.

She's shaking her head. "Not gold. A swan."

"A swan!" I snort. "What kind of romantic disguise is that? What's she going to say, 'Now there's an attractive bird! I'm really into long necks and webbed feet.' I don't think so."

"Persephone! Be quiet!" says Ianthe, the gentle meadow violet. "What if your mother hears you?"

"Let her hear me. I'm not a child anymore. Lots of girls my age are married already."

If only I had the guts to say that to her face.

"I wouldn't want her mad at me," says Kallirhoe. "Drought dries up my stream."

I tug up a long grass and nibble on the softer green at its base.

"So let's hear about this lovesick bird," says Galaxaura, braiding her long white hair. She's a mist-clearing breeze, so she likes to get right to the heart of things.

Kallirhoe lights back up. "He's a rotten husband. Hera's

always watching to see when he's going to go after another woman. He thinks if he disguises himself, she won't know what's happening."

"Like the time he was a bull," says Admete. "I felt sorry for Europa, carried off to sea on his back."

Kallirhoe tosses a handful of pebbles in the water. "Here's what I heard. Zeus had his eye on this mortal named Leda. A really beautiful mortal. He couldn't stop thinking about her. He couldn't even sleep at night. Every time he looked over at Hera, she was staring at him. She knew something was up. But Zeus, being king of the gods, expects to get whatever he wants. There was a lake where Leda always went swimming. And Zeus figured, what's more natural at a lake than a swan? She must have thought he was a pretty attractive swan, because after a while she laid a big egg—"

"No!" We all gasp at the same time.

"Yes! Can you even imagine? How do you think she hatched it?"

My hair is almost dry now. I shake it back from my shoulders. "If he wanted her to go with him, he should have come out and said it."

"Right, and have Hera breathing down his back."

Admete looks disgusted. "You're such a goody-goody, Persephone."

"Am not!" I throw a cupped hand of water at her.

"Are too!" She splashes me back. Soon we're all soaking

wet again, dripping, tangle-haired, lying back on the grass and laughing.

The cool water clears my brain, and for a moment I think I should come out and tell everyone what I saw. I should tell my mother. But then I see his face again, and his hand holding the reins, and the heat starts to soak back into me, evaporating all my good intentions into steam.

Dream

I'm a little girl again. My mother's working close to home, so she lets me come with her.

She takes my hand. We walk to the place where the seeds were just planted. The soil is wet and black. A spade has turned it upside down, so the buried earth meets the sky and the sky brings its breath underground. It feels like I could fall right into that deep, rich place. I crouch, pick up a handful of dirt, and rub it between my fingers. I breathe in the mineral smell of leaves rotting to make a bed for the new. The smell of change.

Then there's a song thrumming through my veins. It's a calling song. Calling seeds to crack open. Calling shoots to push past pebbles and worms. Calling moisture into their roots and up through their stubborn, determined stems.

I realize the song is pulsing through my mother. Her mouth is moving, and the song is in her and from her. But it's more.

She smiles at me. "Do you hear it?"

I lie on the ground and press my ear to the earth. There it is: the steady pulse of roots, the swishy sound of heads uncurling upward. All of it vibrates like the air around a beating drum.

When the song is over and I open my eyes, my mother holds my hand and helps me up. Then she shows me the first one: a tiny spot of brilliant green, so bright I think a piece of the sun is glowing inside. It looks so soft. The round ball at the top is bursting open into leaves, reaching as fast as they can from the soil to the sun.

The Courtyard Gate

I wake up with a strange feeling. Maybe it was seeing my mother smile in that dream. That's how she used to look. But each time she noticed I was taller, her lips grew tighter. And now I look her in the eye.

But I had that dream. Maybe today can be different.

I throw off my covers, open my trunk, and rummage around until I find a wooden box with irises painted on the lid. I take out the golden brooches my mother gave me for my birthday. They're etched with crocuses, poppies, roses—the flowers that grow in our vale. I pull on a chiton and fasten the brooches at my shoulders.

As I walk past her room, I see the goddess clothes spread out on the bed. She must have a festival today. Something flutters in my chest. Maybe, if I ask just right, she'll let me do something for once. Go somewhere. Grow.

It's dark in the shuttered entry hall. I open the door and stand for a minute blinking in hot, bright sun. Then I see her, halfway out the courtyard gate.

She turns back to look at me. She still has on her everyday chiton, and she hasn't put up her hair yet, so it flows behind her like a golden river. Everything about her is graceful: the long, elegant neck, the slender bare feet.

She sighs. "Yes, Persephone?"

I forget what I wanted to say. If there was ever anything to say in the first place.

"Do you need something? Speak quickly," she says. "I'm in a hurry. I have the Thesmophoria, remember?"

I scuff the ground like I'll find words of my own down there below the pebbles.

Another sigh, more impatient this time. "I have to go now, or I won't have time to gather green energy from the vale, and I still need to change. . . ."

Her words hang in the air between us. I grab the last one and throw it back before I can stop myself.

"I want to change, too."

I walk over so she can see my brooches glinting in the sun. "I want to do something new. Something different."

She looks puzzled, then exasperated. "Not now. I have to get ready. Let's talk when I return."

I don't want to let go. "Maybe I could come with you this time."

For a moment she looks like she's going to start a thunderstorm, but then a corner of her mouth twitches, and loosens, and she's actually laughing.

Isn't this what I wanted, to see her smile? So why does my chest feel so tight?

"The idea!" she says, catching her breath. "You at the Thesmophoria!"

"What's so funny about that?"

She sees my face and tamps her laughter down.

"It's my most important festival of the year," she says. "It lasts three days."

"And that's a long time to leave me here," I persist. "Let me come. Maybe I could learn something."

"Do you have any idea—" The last vestiges of her smile disappear. "This is not a game, Persephone. If not for me, crops would wither in the heat. If not for me, rain wouldn't fall gently, nurturing the new seedlings; no, torrents would scour the very soil off the earth. Do you want people to starve?"

What? Where did that question come from?

Her voice gets stronger; she seems to grow taller. "Why do you think mortals build me temples? Why do women leave their homes and spend these three days begging for my blessing before seeds are sown? They want to see plump flesh on their children's bones, that's why. They want grain enough to last the year."

She stops to catch her breath, and actually looks at me for a moment. Her eye lights on the brooches; she takes a step forward, raises her hand, and runs a finger gently over the etched rose at my shoulder. Her voice softens.

"And this is a festival for women, not girls."

"But I'm—"

"No, it's better you not know about certain things. Not just yet." Her hand drops to her side. "And besides, you'd distract me. My work requires constant vigilance. I need to see who deserves rich crops and who should reap a smaller harvest—or even none at all. Mortals are like children; they need our guidance so they can live their lives properly."

I can't help myself. "Right. Like Zeus in his swan outfit."

"What did you say?"

Her face tightens again and wind starts to rustle through the branches. This isn't turning out like I wanted at all.

But she closes her eyes and takes a deep breath, stilling the budding tempest. When she finally looks at me again, I can tell she's forcing herself to be calm.

"Show some sense." She sighs. "At least you can't get into any trouble here."

I almost shout, *I saw a man! Here! In the vale!* But I don't feel like one of her storms. My mouth stays shut.

She turns and walks through the gate, already focused on

gathering the power she needs. Her words trail behind her like ribbons unraveling.

"We can talk in three days, when I return, if you haven't found something to do by then. . . ."

Her voice fades into the grass, her hand reaches up to caress the leaves of a lemon tree, and then she's gone.

At least the house is cool and dark. The last thing I want now is to be outside where she is, in a field somewhere. Communing with the worms.

I pass her door. There's the shimmering chiton splayed out on the bed; and the golden girdle, thick with ripe sheaves of wheat; and the emerald-encrusted crown. Her goddess paraphernalia. Holy of holies.

This time it pulls me in. I walk to the bed. My fingers reach out and touch the luxurious fabric, then sneak underneath so it falls over the back of my hand like a waterfall. Even her weaving is perfect.

Now the rest of my body wants to know how it feels. I glance around, then slip out of my chiton, pick up my mother's dress, and pull it over my head. The fabric floats on, stroking me. I sigh, relaxing into its caress.

Is the girdle light, too? I pick it up. No, it's heavy, solid, resolute. My finger traces the embossed stalks, bumps over the crowded heads of grain. I place it around my waist. The weight grounds me, rooting my feet into the floor. At the same time the airy fabric feels like it's lifting me. I throw my shoulders back, feeling taller.

Then an earthquake shakes the room.

"Persephone!"

Damn. Damn. Damn. What's she doing back already?

"How dare you!"

Outside, wind starts to whip the trees. The room darkens.

"Take that off. Now!"

I pull off the girdle and drop it on the bed. Rip the chiton over my head. Shrink back into my own body.

She grabs the purple fabric and hugs it to her ample breast as if it were her child, not me. Her body trembles with anger.

"Do you have any idea how hard I work to prepare for these mortal festivals?"

Of course I do. She's told me often enough.

I pick up my rough linen and wad it in my hands. We stand for a moment, eye to eye, each of us clutching a chiton.

"You will *never* touch these clothes again. Is that clear?" She waits, almost as if she's expecting an answer. *"I said, is that clear?"*

Why even bother? I turn and walk to my room. I don't look back.

The shutters bang and a last angry gust of wind bursts through, grabbing my hair.

Plum

At the place where the trail forks, I don't even hesitate before turning uphill. I shouldn't stomp so hard; this path grows clearer every day, and I don't want anyone else to see it.

The late-morning heat is working on my anger like fire under a pot.

A quiet, ladylike daughter, that's what she wants. A calm, obedient girl who's happy to stay in one place and out of her way. Well, that's Ianthe, the contented little meadow violet. Not me.

I see the look in my mother's eyes again; I hear her sigh. If I'm such a disappointment, why does she want to keep me here forever? Me, the daughter who can't do anything right.

I hate eternity.

A fat, white cloud hovers above my head, too far from the sun to make any shade. I wish a wind would flare up and grab that cloud's edges, teasing out some wings so it could turn into a griffin and fly away.

I'll lie on my back in the high meadow, that's what I'll do. I'll drown myself in the perfume of that white flower so I don't have to hear her voice anymore.

Better you not know about certain things.

Quiet? Ladylike? Look at these blossoms crowding the path! Roses tumbling all over each other, billowing clumps of irises, daisies and rosemary cramming every spare spot— my mother makes them fling open their petals for every passing bee. There's nothing shy about *them*.

I keep walking and the flowers give way to a dense thicket of plum trees. I'm almost there; I can smell the white flower even here among all this ripening fruit. I reach up to pluck a plum. It's firm and warm from the sun. As the stem snaps, the branch bounces back, and I hear something.

A horse, snorting.

My head jerks up. I take a few steps out from under the leaves.

He's here again. The golden chariot rests in the middle of the field. The four winged horses are nibbling long strands of grass. And he's just standing there, that man, leaning against the chariot. One of his elbows rests on an emblem embossed in gold, a snarling dog with three heads.

Don't run! I will my feet to stay put.

Sun shines full on his face, blazing on the gold behind his night-black hair, making a halo. He's looking right at me.

I've got a second chance and I'm going to use it.

But use it how? What do I do?

My senses are wide open and everything is flooding in: heat, soaking into me so I can feel every single pore opening . . . the sun, burning up the chariot so it looks ready to explode . . . birdsong and the sound of hooves shuffling in the grass. . . .

He smiles. "Hello."

It's a deep voice. I can feel it reverberate in my chest and echo all the way down to my toes.

I know I should leave, but I don't want to. I want to keep my senses like this forever. I'm all eye, all ear, all skin.

His pose may be relaxed, leaning there against the chariot, but I can feel energy radiating from him. And his fingers keep opening and closing again in a wave, as if they're pulling something in.

I try to talk, but no words come out. What am I going to do?

I glance down at the plum in my hand—ripe, purple, and taut with juice—then up at the horses grazing in front of the chariot.

The man must be able to read my mind, because he nods at me.

So very slowly, very quietly, I walk up to one of the horses, the one with a cowlick in his mane. He looks at me with gigantic, black, gleaming eyes. How can such a gentle look come from so much power? His haunches ripple with muscle.

I go slowly, but I don't hesitate.

The horse lifts his shining head halfway and nickers. I come close enough now to touch his neck, but I don't. I hold my hand out, open, the plum resting there. It seems riper than when I plucked it, its darkness reflecting light like the horse's burnished coat. I hold still, waiting.

The horse lowers his neck and takes the plum gently, barely brushing the skin of my palm with his mouth. His breath is warm and damp. It smells like grass and the soil beneath the grass and the rich warmth of his flesh.

Now, while he's chewing, I lift my hand and stroke his neck. It's like the sun is inside that soft black skin.

"His name is Abastor," says the man, and I pull my hand back because for a second I feel like I'm touching him, not the horse.

The man sits down on the edge of the chariot and leans forward, his elbows on his knees, as if to show me I don't have to worry about him coming closer.

"He was the hardest of the four to tame. He has the most spirit, the most independence. He had to choose to be mine."

"Abastor," I whisper, seeing if my voice will work.

He nods. "That's right. The others aren't that particular, or that observant. Wherever we go, whatever we do, is all right by them. But with Abastor, I always watch his ears. I trust what he thinks."

"What is he thinking now?"

"See how relaxed he is, even with you standing close? He's glad we came back."

His calm voice makes me feel braver, so I ask, "Why did you come back?"

"I saw you."

The three words fill every atom of my body so there isn't room for anything else. He's here because of me.

Should I be scared? Because I'm not, with Abastor next to me, and that deep voice rumbling through me with such certainty, and the air thick with perfume, and the sun soaking into my skin, and my mother gone—

"That's why I came," he says, as if it were perfectly normal to cross the cliffs and enter the vale. "This time I was hoping to meet you." He smiles. "Is that all right?"

"Yes." My voice is back to a whisper. "I wanted you to."

He stands and I tense, thinking he's going to walk toward me, but no; he climbs back into the chariot and picks up the reins.

"I have to go," he says. "But I'll come back tomorrow, when the sun is high. Will I see you then?" His words are as thick and rich as honey.

The horses start to unfold their wings. I step back.

"I'll be here," I say.

Above our heads, clouds are starting to move, pulled by some invisible wind.

Secrets

I hear their voices before I see them. Admete's high, care-free laugh floats above Kallirhoe's gentle murmur. I round the trees and Ianthe looks up from a pile of little daisies. She slits a stem with her thumbnail and slides the next one through, making a crown.

Galaxaura holds out her hand and pulls me down next to her on the sand. "Good! Persephone's finally here."

I jerk my hand back, afraid she'll feel how fast my pulse is beating.

Ianthe picks up another stem, then freezes, suddenly alert. "Something else is here, too. Something new."

She closes her eyes in concentration. She looks like an

oracle, reading the future in wisps of temple smoke. Then her eyes pop open.

"Don't you smell it? There's a new flower in the vale."

"Is that all?" Kallirhoe lies back on the warm sand. "I thought for a second it was going to be important."

Ianthe glares at her. "Just because you're a water nymph, you think flowers aren't important? I suppose I'm not that important, either. I'm only a violet nymph. Well, excuse me."

"That's not what I meant, Ianthe. And I can't smell the flowers as well as you can. It's not like they're *my* cousins." Kallirhoe gives an exaggerated sniff. "All I smell is lavender."

"And mint," says Admete, "from up on my mountainside. What about you, Persephone? Can you make it out?"

I close my eyes, trying to focus, trying to be here with my friends, playing their game so they won't look at me too closely or ask where I've been. I take a deep breath.

The flowers are all vying for attention, with my mother's roses winning the competition, as usual. But in a minute I start to tease apart the strands: Admete's mint, and Ianthe's own perfume, and— There it is. As soon as I single out the scent, I see a white flower swaying next to a golden chariot. My eyes fly open like I was pricked with a pin.

Galaxaura laughs. "It must be pretty exciting after all. Look at Persephone, everyone!"

Admete stands up, shaking sand from the folds of her

blue chiton. "Then let's go find it. We'll follow the scent. And Ianthe can greet her long-lost cousin properly."

Admete, with her lithe limbs and bursting energy. Admete, who wants nothing more than to sneak out of the vale and meet men. I imagine her striding right up to the man in the meadow. I imagine him looking her up and down with an appraising eye.

"No!" My voice is too loud. Everyone stares at me. "It's too hot."

"Too hot?" says Galaxaura. "It's not hot."

He's long gone by now; there's nothing for them to find. Except—what if they see the broken stems where his chariot landed? Or what if they find the meadow and fall in love with it because it's beautiful and new, and they come back later, when he's there, and—

"And I'm tired. I just got here."

I close my eyes again, trying to look exhausted. I hear his voice; I feel it pulse in the air around me.

When I open my eyes again, Galaxaura is staring at my face. Sometimes I hate how she seems to see right through me, the same way her breeze clears the lake and leaves it like crystal. I need to distract her.

"No offense, Ianthe," I say, "but I think we should do something more exciting today. We're free as birds. My mother left for three days. She has some big festival, the Thesmo-something."

"Thesmophoria!" cries Admete. "Then she's the one having all the excitement."

"That's it. I asked if I could go. Surprise, surprise; she wouldn't let me."

Admete laughs knowingly. "That's because it isn't for innocent little girls like you."

Let her tease me. She's got their attention now.

She lies back on the sand with a naughty smile. She loves it when everyone is staring at her. "No, it's definitely too much for someone of your tender sensibilities."

"Why?" asks Kallirhoe. "What do the mortals do?"

"What don't they do! They load up carts with enough food and bedding to camp outside town for three days. Women only, mind you, no men. Men would be too shocked to see how their sweet wives commune with Demeter to get a good harvest. That's why women lie and say it's a somber time, so men will let them go."

No men. Why am I not surprised?

"They must use indecent language," prods Ianthe.

"The foulest, and they dance with total abandon, as if Dionysus himself loosed their bonds with his heady wine. It's out of control. And then there are the pigs."

"Pigs?" Kallirhoe is incredulous. "What does that have to do with the harvest?"

"They toss baby piglets into pits for snakes to eat, and haul back up decayed remains from the year before, and mix them with seed grain and prayers to scatter on the earth. Then there are cakes baked in unspeakable shapes, and—"

"What unspeakable shapes?" asks Ianthe, laughing.

"*You* know. It is a fertility festival, after all."

"Wait a minute," I say. "This is my mother you're talking about. She has fits if my dress is too revealing. She won't even let me give up my dolls."

Admete hauls herself back up to sitting and stares at me like I'm an idiot.

"When are you going to realize your mother is one powerful goddess? You only see her here in the vale, where she's the mommy and you're her baby girl. Don't you know what she's capable of? Why do you think everyone is so careful to keep her happy?"

"Hey, I know," says Kallirhoe, sculpting an interesting shape in the sand. "Let's do a little baking ourselves."

Everyone howls with laughter, and I know they've forgotten all about following the new scent.

I look at my crumpled clothes. I think I know where I put my saffron chiton for tomorrow. And my tangled hair needs combing.

I wrap my fingers around a flat, polished stone, hiding it like a secret in the palm of my hand.

Closer

The sun hangs right above my head and the earth swallows my shadow. Everything feels bare, stripped, open. Naked.

I'm scared he'll be there.

I'm scared he won't.

What am I doing, sneaking up the hillside, keeping him secret?

I reach the plum trees and pause, peering out from the branches. There he is, pacing like a panther. The sight of him wakes me up to what I'm doing. *"Men are ruthless and greedy."* I can hear my mother's voice as if she were standing right next to me, whispering in my ear. *"They'll pluck you like a fruit, then toss you aside."*

As if a single male breath would besmirch her realm, tainting it forever. I always thought that was ridiculous. But now—now part of me is frightened. What if this time he grabs me and throws me into his chariot? I can take a step closer—or I can go back home and never see him again. I'd be sitting there weaving dutifully when my mother comes back.

I step out from under the branches.

He looks up at me. I should be smiling or something. Make this look easy. Like I do it all the time.

Even across the meadow his eyes are deep and his hand is opening, reaching forward, and he starts to stride in my direction—

And stops. His hand closes, pulls back, as if he were tugging on reins. All the power that was surging out of him just got reeled back in. Now he sits on the grass, smiles, and says, "I'm glad you came." As if my coming were the most natural thing in the world. I've never felt so confused in my life.

So I sit, too, not right next to him, but an arm's length away, and start rummaging meadow daisies out of the grass so my hands will have something to do.

He reaches his hand forward and I startle. But he just grabs a daisy, breaks it off, and lays it in front of me so I can use it to make my chain. Stem into welcoming stem.

"Abastor knew the way today," he says. "I didn't even need to tell him where we were going."

He must think I'm acting like a skittish horse, because he's speaking with the voice he uses for those gigantic black stallions: soft and certain and full of buried power. It's not so much that I hear his voice; I feel it.

"I know what," I say, looking at my linked flowers. "I'll make this one for you. A daisy crown. But you have to help."

"Me?" He smiles. "I don't think my fingers will work as nimbly as yours."

I glance at his broad hands, then turn quickly back to my work. "I'll do the threading, but I need more flowers."

He leans over to a thick clump of daisies and reaches down, but he stops and waves his hand across the blossoms as if he were clearing away smoke.

"Bees," he says.

"Don't hurt them!" I hold out a hand. Three fat, furred bumblebees stop their irritated circling and fly to my outstretched palm. I lift them to my ear so I can hear their sweet buzzing song.

"Your friends?" he asks, one eyebrow raised.

"Yes. Here, you can listen, too. Hold out your hand."

He lifts up a brown palm. I whisper to the bees and they buzz in return, then fly around him once before settling on his hand.

"Raise it to your ear," I say.

He does, and I see his face gentle as they sing of blossoms opening, of pollen and the laden flight back to the faceted walls of the hive.

He looks at me in wonder as the bees fly away.

I lean back on my hands, laughing, happier than I've ever been before. I look up to the sky and close my eyes, feeling the sun on my face. When I open my eyes again, he's looking at me.

Maybe eternity won't be so bad after all.

By the time I leave, I know I'm not doing anything wrong. He's never going to touch me. Several times he got up and walked over to check on the horses. But he never came any closer to me. So I can come back again tomorrow, and no harm done.

The next day dawns cloudy, the air feels heavy, and the bees are staying safely back in their hives. On my way to the meadow I feel the first drops of soft, warm rain.

He walks to me, takes off his travel cloak, and drapes it over me to keep me dry. Strong, finely woven fabric. I breathe in a multitude of strange new scents—crisp air from above the clouds, far-off pine trees, the dense smokiness of embers—all swirling around me in a dark, warm refuge. The rain is falling harder now.

"Come under the trees," he says. "They'll keep us dry."

But I snuggle the cloak around me and laugh. "Let's stay here. I like the rain."

We sit down in the grass, surrounded by clusters of those intoxicating white flowers; there are so many of them now. Drops gather on his hair, his hands. Warm rain falls harder until rivulets run down his bare shoulders, following the muscled grooves of his arms, and his chiton grows dark with damp and clings to his skin. I stretch out my feet and wiggle my toes in the wet grass and we talk. It's just one more kind of music, like the rainsong, like my hair rubbing against the enveloping cloak, like the gentle clink of the horses' harnesses as they graze nearby.

Words? We pluck them out of the air, stringing them together like daisies in a chain. How wind feels when horses gallop through clouds, that's what he tells me; the gentle tension you need for reins; what you can tell by watching a horse's ears; the lakes beyond these cliffs, reflecting light that shifts so there's no such thing as one blue. And I tell him how flowers sing when they blossom in your hand, and where the bees hide their honey-rich hives—each word joining the last until the chain encircles us like one more sense, as strong as sight or touch.

And then there are the important words. "I'll be here the day after tomorrow," he says, "when the sun is high."

And I say I will, too—

—Even though it gets harder now. Today's the third day. She's coming back.

I'll have to be more careful, that's all. She won't notice. She hardly sees me, anyway. Not the way he sees me, his face intent and alive.

I need to be here. It's not as if I have a choice.

Something to Be Grateful For

"Persephone!" Her voice drifts to my room. "Are you ever going to wake up?"

I drag myself out of bed and down the hall, rubbing the sleep from my eyes, hoping my groggy face, my rumpled hair, will disguise the change in me. She looks up. I needn't have worried.

"I brought you something from the Thesmophoria," she says. "A gift."

I sit down and she pushes an intricately painted box across the table.

"Go on—aren't you going to open it?"

I pull off the top and lift out a lump of pink linen. Out

rolls a terra-cotta pig, fat and confident, a smug expression on its snout.

"There's more! Keep going!"

Yes, another lump is buried in the fabric. I unwrap a terra-cotta piglet, a little squirmy helpless thing looking up with pleading eyes. Pig and piglet. A matched set.

What am I supposed to say? Great toys, Mommy?

"Aren't they wonderful?" Her voice is bright and eager. "The mortals outdid themselves this year. Such a pile of offerings—one of the biggest ever. I was already inhabiting my statue, waiting to be worshiped, and I saw a woman add these. Once the dancing started, I descended and set them aside."

She smiles down at the all-knowing pig and her feeble little piglet, then up at my face. Not seeing anything. Not seeing me.

"I wanted to bring you something special," she says. "I know you've been bored."

I paste on a smile. "Thank you."

She gets up from the table and fills a bowl with figs and walnuts, puts it in front of me, then sits again.

"What a festival!" she says. "I could see the joy in their faces, read it in the looseness of their limbs. How happy women are without men!"

There it is again.

I pick up a fig and cradle it in a cupped hand. "You really hate men, don't you?"

"I don't hate them. It's just that they're . . . irrelevant."
She's getting that I'm-imparting-knowledge look. "True
power lies in the womb, nurturing seeds and sheltering life."

She reaches across the table to lift a stray lock of hair from
my eyes and tuck it behind my ear. My hand tightens around
the fig.

She sees my hair; she doesn't see me. Doesn't see I'm not
the same person she left three days ago. Doesn't smell the
new scents his cloak left in my hair, or feel the warmth rising
from my skin, or hear the difference in my heartbeat.

Good.

"But men are useful for some things, aren't they?"
I ask. "You needed one to start me. I wasn't exactly self-
seeding."

She's in such a good mood, she laughs as if my question
were a joke between us.

"Yes, a man 'started' you, and then I found us a home
far from men's bullying selfishness, their restraints, their
demands."

She rests a long, cool hand on my arm. I try not to pull
away. And then I surprise myself by saying, "Who was my
father?"

It's a question I stopped asking years ago, once I noticed
how her eyes always narrowed and how quickly she changed
the subject. But this time she gives me what she'd probably
describe as a look of understanding.

"Your father? What does it matter? He saw no reason to be involved in your life." She sits back. Something occurs to her and she smiles. "And I suppose that means he gave us *one* thing to be grateful for: his absence! Let's not talk about him again. There's no need."

No need. And so there's no need to tell her about the last three days, either.

I stand and wrap the pigs back in their pink shroud.

Grateful? Well, she gave me something to be grateful for, too. And it wasn't these ridiculous pigs. She made it as clear as sunlight that I need to keep my secret. She's incapable of understanding why I'd want a man in my life.

I put the lump in the box and fasten the lid. There won't be any thunderstorms as long as she doesn't know.

"Thank you," I say again.

And she beams back at me, so happy we've had this little talk.

Ripples

"Where have you been all morning?" calls Kallirhoe. "Come over here fast. Admete's got news."

They're all staring at her, which is great. This way they won't peer at me. I must look as different as I feel. It's like I used to be a stunted shoot and now that I've had my first taste of rain, I'm sprouting bright green leaves all over the place. How would I explain it to them? A good night's sleep?

Then I get close enough to see Admete's face and I know. She's in love.

"When you told us your mother was away," she says, "I decided to go exploring."

"Wait!" says Ianthe, looking around like an anxious

sparrow. "Don't say it again until we're in the rowboat." She gets up and pulls over the old, flat-bottomed scow, and we all pile in. Kallirhoe pushes us off toward the middle of the lake, then settles down with one leg draped over the side so her toes make ripples.

"All right," says Ianthe, relaxing and turning her face to the sun, "go on, Admete. Start over from the beginning."

"I was exploring and I found something I never noticed before—a place where my stream flows near a crevice in the cliff. It would be too small for any of you to squeeze into, but I was able to trickle through, and I wanted to see what was on the other side."

She looks like she's melting, boneless, against the hull of the boat. "There's a path. It goes all the way to the ocean, to a hidden little cove. And he was there."

"He?" Has she seen him, then, in his chariot, his four black horses?

"Stop wobbling the boat, Persephone. He's a river god, with blue-green skin and wave-green eyes. He's young and strong, and when he whispered in my ear . . ." Her lids droop, as if all her energy is getting sucked inside, to the place where her heart is beating.

Kallirhoe gives an appreciative sigh. Even Ianthe looks dreamy. I relax and trail my fingers in the lake, sketching lines for a moment before they disappear into nothing again.

Then Galaxaura blows the mood away with a blast of reality. "What does your father say?"

"My father? You think I'd tell him?" Admete gives a hard little laugh. "Once he remembers I'm here, he'll marry me off like he did with my sisters. I'll get some stodgy old man with a great pedigree. Someone who's already gray. And flabby." She shudders. "No, the second my father finds out, that's the end of my fun."

Ianthe glances around again. "And what about Demeter? What if she hears you've been lying?"

"Calm down, Ianthe," I say. "Admete isn't exactly lying; she's just neglecting to mention something. It's different."

Ianthe shakes her head. "I think you should be careful, that's all. Deception sows some dangerous crops."

She doesn't understand. You can't always tell everyone everything. Sometimes you have to cheat, just a little tiny bit, to get what you want. It won't hurt anybody.

Admete isn't really listening to us. She takes a deep breath and closes her eyes, and it's obvious she's with her river god again. "It was quiet except for lapping waves, and moonlight was dancing on the water, and when he kissed me . . ."

The rest of us lean so far in her direction, the boat tilts.

"Tell us!" begs Kallirhoe.

But Admete doesn't say another word. She's lost in a moonlit cove, blue-green arms wrapped around her glistening skin.

Beneath the Earth

We sit closer. His hand is only a few inches from mine on the grass. He's wearing a golden ring with that three-headed dog on it, the same snarling beast that guards his chariot. I want to trace the raised outline.

He still hasn't touched me.

"Why do you come here, really?" I ask.

"You intrigue me, Persephone."

He seemed to know my name from the start; I suppose I told it to him. When he says, "Persephone," his deep voice flows all around me, warm, like a caress.

But do I know his name? No—and what's more, I haven't even asked him. I've had plenty of chances. Maybe I'm afraid if I say his name, reality will come crashing into this dream world where we meet. I'll keep him a dream if it means I can be with him longer.

There's so much I don't know.

"How far do you travel to get here?" I ask.

"Oh, a long, long way. It's another world, really."

"You come from the stars just to visit me?"

He laughs and his smile is so real, so alive, I feel like the whole vale is suddenly lit up.

"My home is in the other direction. I come from down here, beneath the earth." He smooths the long grass with his fingers, and his voice seems to resonate through the soil and the rock and the fire beneath the rock at the center of the earth. I burrow my fingers under the grass, as if I could find the path of his voice there, among the roots.

He tilts his head, giving me a piercing look. "What do you think of that?"

"It must be wonderful," I say. "That's where this all starts growing, after all. Down there in that rich darkness."

He looks inordinately pleased. "I'm glad to hear that."

His fingers find an errant fold in the cloth of my chiton and they start to stroke it. Everything tingles—the air, my skin. I can feel molecules of desire floating around me, traveling up the threads in the cloth so they hug my whole body.

"Let me tell you something," he says. "Not everyone agrees with you about my home. They like this part of existence: green leaves, fresh petals. But this soil . . ." He drops the cloth to pull up a handful of earth, letting the moist black grains sift through his fingers. "This comes from leaves and trees long past. Everything dies, and dying, returns to earth, air, water, and fire. To start again. Where I come from."

I want his hand back on my chiton. I want it to touch me through the cloth.

I try to keep my voice steady. "That's the problem here. Everything's green, everything's female, everything's the same. This flower . . ."

I reach out to a stalk leaning toward me and run a finger across its bulging bud; it's so ripe, the bud splits at my touch and white petals start to unfold right in front of us with a burst of perfume. I snap its stem and take a long, deep breath.

"Funny," I say, "I don't even know its name."

"Narcissus."

"This narcissus needs the earth below as much as it needs the sun."

"I was hoping you'd say that," he says, suddenly all seriousness. There's such a coiled intensity in his gaze, I have to pull my eyes away. Then, looking only at the flower, I hold it out to him. He lifts his hand and wraps it around my hand around the stem. He starts to pull my hand toward him, starts to pull me toward him—yes, I think, yes—and then he stops.

"Wait," he whispers, as if to himself. He unfolds his fingers and gently lifts the flower from my hand. He puts it inside the drape of his chiton, next to his skin.

"There's something we need to talk about," he says. "But I have to leave now. Come back tomorrow." His eyes are ablaze. "Tell me you'll come."

"Yes. I'll come."

I drag my feet back along the path. I'm as slow and heavy and full of heat as the olive trees. With every step I play his voice in my head again, the way fingers keep playing the same tune on the strings of a lyre. I'm putting his hand on my hand over and over and over.

Talk? He knows what I want. I want him to kiss me. Why do we need to talk?

A snake slithers off the path and disappears under some tree roots.

At least I know something more about him. He lives underground, so he's probably a river god. I try to picture his home and I see an echoing cave, dripping with stalactites. I hear a surging river, as dark as his hair. It might be under my feet right now.

Roses crowd the path, but I don't smell them. I smell narcissus.

I bet that three-headed dog roams his lands, scaring off mortals who sneak in to steal gemstones and fat veins of gold.

I'll ask him tomorrow. I'll ask him his name.

I drift around the last bend, a boat on the stream of my thoughts. The lemon trees float into view, and then the red clay roof tiles, lapping each other like waves, and the white-plastered walls, the shutters closed against the heat.

And my mother, pacing.

Her short, crisp steps block the courtyard gate. Her arms are crossed as tight as prison walls. She whirls at the end of a step, and her eyes meet mine.

A Grave Concern

She knows. It's the only thing that would explain the tension in her shoulders, the straight slash of her mouth, the hunter's eyes. She must have been there at the edge of the meadow, maybe saw his hand touching mine, the narcissus, the look in his eyes, my hand lingering. . . .

I'm dead. Dead. Dead.

"Persephone."

Her voice is a command. I drag my feet toward her, wishing I could turn and run. My hand clutches at the lavender bushes as if they could swallow me, but my feet keep walking, step by agonizing step.

She isn't pacing anymore, just standing there, staring, waiting.

I pass a tree. *Open your rough bark*, I pray silently. *Close me in*. Nothing.

How long has she known?

As I approach she lifts her hand and I cringe. But she's just motioning me into the courtyard and then to a stone bench. I sit.

She draws a deep breath, looking down at me. I look at the hands clenched in my lap.

I'll never see him again.

"I've heard news that causes me grave concern." Her voice is as rigid as her lips. "It would be an understatement to say I'm disappointed in you."

My cheeks are burning; my heart is pounding so loud, I have to struggle to hear her words.

She takes a few steps and stares over the gate, her eyes tracing the path. "I have always allowed you considerable freedom. I haven't asked you to tell me where you're going or which friends you see. I have felt, in the security of this vale, I need not limit you to our four walls. Now I doubt the wisdom of my choice."

My body is an empty shell. That's all I'll ever be now: a husk, rattling in the wind.

He'll wait for me tomorrow, maybe the next day, maybe one more, and then he won't come back.

I barely sense her sitting next to me. She lifts my hand from my lap, traps it between her cool fingers.

"Yet what happened is certainly not your fault, nor, other than neglecting to tell me, are your own actions in question. So it is clearly not you who should be punished."

What?

"And so I have asked Admete to leave," she says, dropping my hand. She stands again, paces a few steps, and heaves a vast sigh, rustling the leaves. "To think I've been nurturing this traitor in my vale! I must tell you, when I heard she had been seeing this . . ."—she stops, shudders—"this so-called 'river god,' I was shocked. There has . . ."

Her words wash over me, nothing but noise. She doesn't know!

". . . and in the future I would expect you to tell me when you hear news of inappropriate . . ."

The orchestra inside me drowns out her voice. It's playing a song of sun and skin, blaring about the life filling me again. I'm thinking of the way his hand looked lying on the grass, the brown back of his hand, the sunlit hairs licking his glowing arm.

A New Pattern

The afternoon hangs hot and endless. I'm working at my loom in the courtyard, under the shade of the overhang. The warp threads, pulled taut by their silver weights, are blue like the sky after twilight, when night deepens its hold. I've just started on the background. The fabric is smooth and free of blemish. I run my finger down the suspended threads. They're waiting to see what life I'll weave into them.

Plain blue would be too simple. Where's the art in that? I used to weave fabric without pattern when I was little, back and forth, back and forth, learning to get the tension even. But now I know what I'm doing. First, a border. I pick up the black yarn. It's mysterious against the blue, like a shadow at night. I start with horses running across the top of the fabric. It's coming so easily today; I'm weaving them as smoothly as the fates weave mortal lives, measuring out the length of their thread, the number of their days.

Over the sounds of fountains and birds, I hear steady footsteps. My mother must be on her way to the groves. Now that she's cautioned me, she wants to be friends again. She comes over to look at my work and smiles with rare approval.

"You've learned well. This is a gracious design. I can almost feel the wind under their feet. And your colors are pleasingly subtle."

Then she's gone across the paving stones, under the fig trees and out of sight.

I could stop now if I wanted. I've done enough. I should find my friends down by the lake because we need to talk about Admete. But something's tugging at my fingers.

I reach down to the basket of wools and rummage around. There it is, near the bottom, a golden yellow. Why is it calling me? What does it want to become? It's the color of the sun, but I don't want the sun against this deep, dark blue. Maybe a row of flowers.

I wind the golden wool on a shuttle and start a first row, hints of gold for the pointed tips of petals, getting ready to work my way down. Row follows row and the rhythm lulls me.

The shuttle wants to pull my hand. Maybe I'll just let it have its way.

The golden shapes grow wider. Now they look like pointed ears, six of them. I follow them down to bold eyes. I've seen this before: three heads, one staring right at me and the others turning to guard each side. I've brought the three-headed dog from the chariot to life. There's an energy in him, a fierceness and alertness, that almost frightens me. I've never woven so well.

It must be hours later when my mother comes humming back into the courtyard. I hope she stops to look again and admire my work. I keep weaving, pretending I don't see her so she won't think I care. She comes over. I'm already smiling for her praise.

"Persephone!"

Her voice sets off alarms in my head.

"What on earth are you doing? Where did you see that?"

I think fast. "It felt like it was weaving itself, like in a dream." That part is true, after all. I just won't say the rest, about the chariot with the design in gold and the meadow full of narcissus.

"A dream? Are you sure that's all? Because if Cerberus is here in the vale—" She looks ready to smite someone.

I'm scared and excited and my body is tingling, because I can tell this is huge. I have to know why.

I make my eyes wide. I shake my head like an innocent

little girl. "I've never seen a living creature like this, I swear." True again, as far as it goes. "Who is it? What does it mean?"

"That brute roams the banks of the Styx."

"The Styx?"

"You know," she says crossly. "The river separating the earth from the underworld, the realm of Hades. I gather this beast is *his* special friend: Dark Hades, ruler of one-third of all creation, the insatiable lord of the dead."

I gasp. It's him.

I must be turning pale because she nods and says in a gentler voice, "I know. Death, decay—they make me shudder, too. I don't know why your dreams sent this image, but it doesn't belong here. Just pull out the threads and start over. No harm done."

I barely hear her. I need to know more. "Have you been there?"

"The underworld? Certainly not. It's closed to all the gods but Hermes, who guides mortal shades to its borders. Hermes—and his companion Death."

"What's it like?"

"Stop it," she says, as if she were talking to a toddler. "This morbid curiosity is unbecoming in a girl." She waves a hand toward the gate and the groves beyond. "*This* is your world: olives, lavender, poplars, figs. This is all you need to know. You're safe here. Undo this weaving now, and all will be well."

Undo it? My best work ever?

"But Mother, the eyes, the teeth, aren't they good? Can't you see the power in them?"

"You don't need that kind of power."

She snatches the shuttle from my hand and starts to pull out the golden thread. Row by row. Soon the blazing eyes will be gone forever.

"Don't!"

I grab her hand and try to pull out the shuttle. She's got it by both hands now and she's pulling and I'm pulling. Her breath is short and her eyes are blasting fire, and here come those damn thunderclouds on the horizon and that stupid wind carrying the scent of rain, and *I don't care*. I won't let go.

"Give it to me!" I shout.

"Never!"

With one hand I'm holding the yarn, trying to keep it in the weaving, and with the other I'm grabbing the shuttle, and then—snap!—the yarn breaks and my mother and I tumble back out of the shade into the glaring sun. We're both panting, staring at each other. She's won the shuttle with the golden thread. She looks at it with disgust, then throws it on the ground. She stalks into the house.

I'll pay for this later. I know I will. The wind is so strong this time. But even in its threat, it carries the smell of the lake, and something else. Something sweeter. The scent of narcissus, blowing over from the meadow.

I go back under the overhang into the cool shade. The loom is a wreck. The fabric is snagged, the remnants of the pattern pulled askew. And all the hanging threads, the ones that show you where you're going, are tangled.

Lord of the Maggot

She appears at my door, all golden hair and floating white dress.

"You may leave your room now. I hope this experience has taught you a lesson."

"Yes, Mother. I'm sorry."

Anything she wants to hear, I'll say. Anything that will get me back to the meadow before another day goes by.

All yesterday I was trapped in this room, watching the sun rise, and peak, and set. Staring out the window with nothing to do but repeat his name over and over and over. Hades, Lord of the Dead.

The name he never told me. And I know why. Again, I

picture Leda and her amorous swan, and a bitter taste fills my mouth.

"I think I'll go down to the lake," I say, feigning indifference, "if that's all right with you."

She stands aside to let me pass. "Yes. Thank you for letting me know."

I stroll out the door and down the path, trying to look nonchalant.

The air is stifling, full and floral, and I want to clear it away with a knife. I glance back. The house is out of sight, so I walk faster.

Hades. Ruler of every mortal shade and one-third of all creation. I intrigue him, do I? My hands clench into fists.

We have some talking to do.

I burst past the plum trees into the meadow. Hades is sitting on the edge of his chariot, smiling. Then he sees my face and stands. Abastor looks over and flicks his ears warily.

"I know who you are." My voice is as taut as an overstretched rope.

"Good."

How can he look so calm? He takes a step toward me; I take two back.

"Good?" My fists tighten at my sides. "How can you say that? You never even told me your name, and now I know why! You were deceiving me! Letting me think you were some river god, just like Zeus with his little disguises. You were lying!"

He shakes his head, but his eyes stay on mine. "I never lied to you."

He walks up to me and takes my hand, trying to open my fingers. I yank my hand back.

"Nothing is complete with just one side," he says, pressing closer. "You said so yourself. You stroked the earth as if you heard it calling from below. But now that you know who I am, you fear me, hate me, like all the rest of them. And you wonder why I waited to tell you my name?"

Now his face is only inches from mine; his words, relentless.

"I'm used to scorn. Gods and mortals alike shun what they can't see. They don't want to think about the fragile thread binding body to soul. They hear a sick woman's wail and they think of me. They bury a maimed soldier and they think of me. They call me lord of the maggot and rotting flesh. And you wonder why I waited to tell you my name?"

He pauses, lifting a tender hand to my cheek. When he speaks again, his voice is suddenly intimate. "But I thought you, and you alone, understood. I heard you say it yourself: everything needs change. Life needs death to quicken against. Yes, I waited to say my name, waited for you to know me as I am. But how can you say I deceived you?"

I'm starting to melt toward his hand. I force myself to

turn away, gathering my anger around me like armor. Then I whirl back to face him.

"Why don't you go try that smooth voice on someone else?" I say. "Fear? No! But if I'd known who you are, I would have seen the rest of it, too. You're not serious about me! No, a lord like you—with a third of all existence to rule—you need a *real* queen by your side. Someone who knows about power, and palaces, and the ways of mortals and gods!"

I glance down at my bare feet, my simple linen chiton. Then I glare back up into his eyes.

"There I was, just floating along on your charm, all innocent, not thinking beyond the next second by your side, the next touch of your hand. But as soon as I heard your name . . ." My voice drops low, a whisper of breeze in the storm's lull. "That's when I knew you'd never take me with you. And I realized that's what I wanted all along."

How *dare* he smile? The storm whips up again. I step closer, my fist raised to pound on his chest, and now I'm shouting at him: furious, humiliated, devastated by my loss.

"So you've been playing with me, that's all! Waiting for me to ripen, like a plum, until I was ready to kiss you—or more!—and then you'd be gone. As if I were a toy! A game! That's it, isn't it? Well, isn't it?"

He doesn't answer, just grabs me. And then he's pressing into me, wrapping me in arms as strong as bronze, and his

mouth is on mine, hot and hungry, filling me until everything else disappears—the meadow, my anger—and this is
all I want. It's all I want forever.

"Persephone." His voice is soft and deep and endless. "I came
here for one reason only: to ask you to be my queen."

He runs a broad hand down my back, and when it's at the
base of my spine, he pulls me even closer. He chuckles softly
in my ear. "Do you know how hard it was for me to wait? I
wanted to toss you in that chariot the moment I saw you and
finish convincing you later."

Yes, I think. Kiss me now; convince me later.

He tilts his head so he can look in my eyes. "But I
couldn't. You had to know me first as a man, not a god.
Because you have to choose to come with me. Otherwise
your power might not survive the crossing, and I'd be a fool
to risk losing that. I want all of you."

"My power?"

I must look confused. He gently loosens his hold.

"Let me show you something."

He raises a hand and points at a tree by the meadow's
edge. In front of my eyes, the tree turns brown: leaves shrivel
and flutter and fall in piles, branches crack and shatter on
the ground, the trunk collapses into fragments and dissolves
into swirling motes of dust. A few seconds, and it's gone.

Two brown leaves settle near my feet.

Hades looks at me carefully. "That's my realm. Death."

I pick up one of the shriveled leaves and rub it between my fingers.

"But you!" he says eagerly. "You have the opposite power, a bursting green energy, the power in the fresh shoot just starting to uncurl."

I shake my head, but he keeps going.

"Together, we make the cycle complete. And that means more power than either of us has alone. No, I don't need a sophisticated goddess, and neither does my realm. I need you."

He lifts my hand and unfolds my fingers. The edge of the leaf is tinted with the slightest shimmer of green.

"But that happens all the time," I protest. "It's just the vale! The power you want, the energy—that's my mother, not me."

"Does your mother have these eyes?" he asks, his hand near my temple. I shake my head. "This lithe body?" The hand runs down my side. "This mouth?" His finger traces my lips. Again I shake my head.

"Then I'll take my chances," he says. "Because you're the one I want."

The next kiss sweeps the world clean away—his arms enveloping me, his breath filling me, the feel of his skin and his mouth and his beard and his hands. . . .

"Come with me now," he murmurs in my ear. "Be my queen. I'll set a golden crown on your raven hair."

A crown? Me?

He sees my expression and laughs. "Don't worry. Ruling is easy. I'll teach you." He pauses, then adds, "But there is one more thing I should tell you. When you come, there's no returning to Earth. It's forever."

Forever. I don't like that word.

"I don't see why," I say. "Hermes crosses back and forth when he wants."

"Not when he wants; when he has souls to guide."

Abastor snorts impatiently. Hades glances up. He puts his arm behind me and turns me firmly in the horse's direction.

"Some things I can't control," he continues. "I can't come to Earth whenever I want, either. The rules stretched so I could fetch you home; they won't bend again." He starts guiding me toward the chariot. "And what's the need? We want to be with each other, forever."

He's in total command, so sure of what he wants. So sure what I should do—

No! This time I'm going to make my own choice. I stop and he has to stop with me.

"I need time to think," I say.

"Don't think too much." He leans in close so his soft voice fills me. He knows his power. "Come now."

His words pull me in, his arms enfold me; my body is already saying yes. But somehow I reach deep and find enough brain to say, "Tomorrow I'll tell you yes or no."

The Journey

I move away from the dark window and slide two brooches from my shoulders, weighing one in each hand.

This one—the one in this hand is my bed, the same bed I've slept in forever. It's my trunk, my mirror with a handle shaped like Aphrodite, these covers I wove. It's Kallirhoe's gentle stream and Ianthe's perfume. It's the way the air sparkles when Galaxaura blows the mist away.

And the other—the other hand feels light with not knowing. What is it like down there in the underworld? Dark, smoke-filled caverns, maybe, lit by flickering torches and filled with moaning, writhing human souls? He called them shades—I bet they don't even look human anymore. How does anyone rule over puffs of smoke? I should have asked. I seem to be good at not asking.

I drop my closed palms to my sides and walk the six steps to the other wall, turn, and walk back, trying to imagine a crown on my head.

But Hades is no phantom. He's solid and real. He's what matters, not all the rest. I close my fingers tighter around that brooch, and now both hands are weighted as I walk and turn, walk and turn.

It's much later when my mother passes the door and sees me pacing. A line of concern wanders across her brow.

"Is something the matter?" she asks.

"The matter? Nothing's the matter."

I try to wash all the feelings off my face and leave it as clear as the lake.

"It's late, past your bedtime. Why are you still up? Something must be troubling you. Let me help."

She has a hopeful expression, almost pitiful in its eagerness for me to let her in. She's really trying. I know she is.

But if I tell her . . .

His kiss sweeps over me again, so strong I have to struggle to stay on my feet. If I tell her, that's what I'm giving up: that kiss, those eyes burning into me. Not to mention any chance of ever living my own life.

"Is it Admete, dear? Is that what's bothering you?"

And then I know. I've made up my mind.

"Your cheeks are flushed." She walks over and places her cool palm on my forehead. "You should spend tomorrow in bed, resting."

She pulls back the coverlet and steps aside for me to lie down. She pulls the covers up to my chin. "Sleep is what you need."

I let her kiss my brow. Then it hits me: this is it. I'll never see her again. I grab her hand and press it to my cheek.

"Well!" she says, smiling. "Good night, Persephone."

Softly, too softly for her to hear, I whisper, "Good-bye."

Across the field in morning sunlight, hugging the trees and vines, slipping into their shadows, staying far from the path that passes by Kallirhoe's stream. I hear laughter down by the lake, the splash of an oar, voices rising and falling like ripples. I hurry in the other direction. They mustn't see me, call to me, ask me where I'm going. Up ahead, where the olive and plum trees open into meadow, I see the glare of light reflecting off gold. The chariot. Black horses grazing, their glossy coats shining in the sun. And Hades, pacing.

The narcissus have grown so thick now, blossoms crowd around his feet. Their scent pulls me from under the plums' dense leaves and I step from dappled light into full sun.

The horses flick their ears. Hades lifts his head and pivots, alert.

And then he's walking toward me, eyes fixed on me as if I

were prey. Unsmiling. All jaw, cheekbone, shoulder.

I'm frozen.

He walks toward me, fine-spun cloth outlining his thighs, stroking golden brown skin, and a breeze is playing with my hair, brushing my arm—

He walks toward me, easy, as if he owned me.

The air around me is heating. Energy crowns him like a halo, emanates from his arm, his hand—

Walks toward me.

Don't stop! Nothing is safe. I don't want it to be. So what if I'm changing my life forever? Forever is this one instant, when he's almost here.

He sees what's in my eyes. He reaches me and grabs me, pulls me close. His mouth on my mouth. His scent mingling with the flowers' intoxicating perfume. The strength of his arms.

There is no way I could pull myself back from this eternity. But he does. Pulls back, looks me in the eyes, and says in a husky voice, "Tell me you're coming with me. Say you'll be my queen. Say it."

It's easy. I'm drunk, drugged on narcissus and skin. No doubt. This isn't my home. His arm will be my home. His skin will touch me and that is all I need.

I nod.

"Say it out loud," he says. "Say you choose to come with me."

"Yes," I say. "I choose to come."

Hades lifts me into the chariot as if I weighed no more than a lamb being carried to market. He leaps up beside me; the horses snort and paw the earth, tossing their heads. Then he snaps the reins and the horses start running like water breeching a dam, sudden, unstoppable. There's a jolt, and their mighty legs are galloping through air.

We soar above plum trees and olive groves, above the lake, where a rowboat, unmoored, floats empty in the middle. The air rushing past me becomes a wind, blowing my hair and the folds of my chiton behind me like wings.

Suddenly, a phalanx of pink stone rises in front of us, blocking out the world—the cliffs, trying to hold me in. But with one forceful stroke, the horses carry us right over my prison walls.

For the first time, I see the world outside the vale: paths leading down to coves murmuring with waves, rich jumbles of fields, white-walled villages, tiny specks of sheep on green hillsides, and lakes glinting blue and green like precious gems.

Everything shrinks smaller and smaller, until the trees are green dots, and then even the dots disappear and there's nothing below us but bold strokes of paint: green, brown, gold.

Hades snaps the reins, urging the horses as fast as they'll go. The wind becomes an exhilarating gale, rocking the chariot side to side, and my knuckles turn white on the golden rail, holding on, just holding on. Hades' cloak snaps and cracks behind us with the sounds of raging fire.

Then down, without slowing. Green rushes toward us, gives way to rocky, barren land, and then everything is white and we're plunging into clouds that seem to rise from the earth itself. No, not clouds, steam, billowing up with a sulfurous smell, and we're plummeting right into that shifting, swirling mass as if the ground is pulling open. We plunge through a cleft in the rock, and all I can do is hold on tighter as the chariot rocks and hot steam roils about us. That's all there is: steam, wind, the chariot careening from side to side; and a scream rips out—is it mine?—and even that sound disappears, sucked into the swirling, thick air, and I hold on and I hold on. There is nothing but holding on.

PART TWO
Below

Who were you? It's gone. You can't remember.
The room you grew up in, the tree outside your window,
the shadows of its branches waving on the wall.
Gone.

Shutters

There's darkness all around me, an ocean of it. And I'm adrift in a raft of a bed.

"Hades?" I whisper.

Nothing. No answer.

"Hades? Where are you?"

I reach blindly across the bed, but no matter which way I grope, I find no reassuring arm, no broad shoulder to shake.

I don't believe it! He's left me alone to the dark.

To the dark—and what else? I shiver into fine-spun sheets and strain my ears, trying to hear something, anything. What sounds do shapeless wraiths make? Do they even speak once they leave their mortal bodies, or are they only wavering bits of mist? And where are those flickering torches I was counting on to give me light?

When Hades talked about the darkness beneath the earth, I didn't think he meant *this*.

"Hades? Anybody?"

As if in answer to my call, a faint golden rectangle emerges from the darkness, floating like four lines sketched with a glowing ember. Like a door.

I scoot to the side of the bed and swing my feet down until they meet cold, polished stone. My arms outstretched like a sleepwalker, I totter toward the glimmering outline. One careful step, two, three, four . . . and then my fingers touch wood.

Shutters! The golden rectangle is a window frame!

I fumble the latch open, and the room floods with glorious, blinding light. The sun, here in the underworld! That's the last thing I expected to find. I blink until I can make out sky and hills covered with tawny grass.

No smoky caverns, no dripping stalactites—I sigh with relief. Maybe I can handle this after all.

Now I can see the room. The bed looks like it's carved from the trunk of a single, gigantic tree. Sinuous roots, polished to a rich red-brown, disappear into the floor, as if slurping up nourishment from the land below. It's gorgeous.

But the rest of the room reels with gaudy decorations: frescoed deer cavort on the walls, geometric mosaics dance underfoot, spirals and rosettes swirl across a distant ceiling like the leaves of some towering tree. I could fit ten of my bedrooms in here. I could fit my entire courtyard.

I wrap myself in a sheet, shuffle over, and open two more windows. Below me stretches a hill speckled with rocks and bushes. Halfway down, a broad oak beckons. And farther still, there's a curving strip of green where trees—tiny from this distance—trail leafy fingers in a river. People are swimming. Well, not people; shades, I suppose. But even from this distance they look distinctly human, not wraithlike at all.

The scrub grass calls to me. We never had brown grass in the vale. I need to see how it feels under my feet. And those squat, scraggly bushes—I want to rub their leaves, lift my fingers, and breathe in their scent.

But where's Hades? Last night it felt like he'd never leave my side again. And now . . .

Well, if he can go off alone, I can, too. I straighten my shoulders, firming up my courage. I'm going to explore my new home. All I need is my clothes.

I look across the polished floor, but it's bare. A row of wooden chests lines the wall across from the windows. Maybe Hades tossed my chiton in there.

I throw open the first trunk. Mountains of jewels glare

out at me: diamonds, lapis, rubies, amber, little white pearls and black pearls the size of olives, and a huge golden crown slashed with rubies. A necklace dangles emeralds as fat as green plums. I run my fingers through the glittering treasure.

The second trunk is a tangle of shoes, with spun-silver laces, and diamonds encrusted like barnacles, and three-headed dogs worked in golden filigree. I slip the last pair on under my sheet. They fit perfectly, as if they were made for me. But I catch myself. If I spend all morning getting lost in this stuff, I'll never feel the grass under my feet. I toss the shoes back and drop the lid.

Finally, in the third trunk, I find chitons—dozens and dozens of them. A tumble of color grows at my feet as I pull them out, searching for mine: saffron, persimmon, gold, a deeper purple than my mother's finest. And the decorations, the patterns! Silver seashells scattered on ocean blue, black-winged horses flying over grass-green linen. Palace gowns, far too grand for a barefoot stroll.

One yellow dress looks plainer than the rest. I slip it on. Once I belt the waist, the hem skims the tops of my feet, just the way I like it.

Then I see the brooches are marked with the letter *P.* So is the girdle.

I grab some necklaces from the jewelry trunk and dump them on the bed. There it is on the clasps: *P.* And woven into the hem of the grass-green chiton. And the blazing ruby crown—yes, here it is.

Of course. They're mine.

"Queen Persephone," I say out loud, and my voice echoes in the vast room.

The crown is too heavy in my hands; I fling it on the growing pile with a shiver.

Wait a minute. What am I nervous about? Any of my friends would love to have these clothes. And when it comes time to wear them, Hades will help me learn my way around. What was it he said? "Ruling is easy. I'll teach you."

I take a deep breath. Right now I'm going to discover my new home and its grasses, its leaves, its trees. I'll find my way down to that river and go for a swim. Then I'll come back, find Hades, and ask how he could leave me to wake up alone.

The halls twist and tangle like octopus arms, and there must be thousands of rooms: reception rooms with gilded couches, and storage rooms stacked with trunks and ampho-rae of wine or oil, and warrens of workrooms. I pass the same red marble bathtub four times.

Then I glance down a hall. Finally! There's Hades, stand-ing with his hand on the three-headed dog's back. I run up, but he stands still and unmoving— Damn. It's only a statue, frozen forever in painted marble.

But the statue is next to a stair, and at the bottom of the stair is a door, and the door leads me out into bright morning sunlight.

And there are people everywhere.

Shades, I remind myself, shades. But they look as solid as I do, and their voices ring in the air, and I can hear their feet pattering across the stone forecourt. You couldn't tell they were different from me just by looking.

Then I see two of them heading right toward me: a gray-haired man and an elegant younger woman, their eyes respectfully lowered, their steps slow and thoughtful. They know who—what—I am!

My breath comes in short, shallow bursts. The shades are already worshiping me! I don't know how to do this! I don't know how to be a queen yet; nobody's told me anything! And I didn't even dress up like I probably should have, not a single piece of jewelry. I bet I was supposed to wear a crown. Soon they'll be close enough to kneel before me on the hard stones. What do I *do*? My head is scrambling. I try to picture my mother. She'd never bow—maybe tilt her head in acknowledgement? That's it. I'll tilt my head. And my voice will fail me if I try to speak, I know it will—I'll have to use my hands to bid them rise. Oh, *why* didn't I wait for Hades to come?

I straighten the folds of my chiton, pull my shoulders down, and prepare to incline my head.

The man nods at me. "Good day," he says, and the woman smiles as they pass right by. Right by, on their way to a bench a few steps behind me. They sit and start talking to each other.

I deflate like the throat of a bullfrog all done croaking.

All that panic for nothing! I look down at my bare feet, my plain chiton, my ringless hands. They must think I'm one of them. Being a queen seems to be all in the clothes.

I walk near a group of young women with their arms around each other's waists. Carefully covering the *P* on my brooch, I smile and say hello. They grin back and one beckons. I wave my hand but keep walking.

It's true, then. No one knows who I am!

Relief floods through me. I don't have to be a queen right away. If I dress like this, I can learn bit by bit, and in between I can be as normal as any mortal.

The Lethe

I walk out of the forecourt, and soon I'm on my own again. Rough brown grass tickles my feet. I pluck a few blades and roll them between my fingers. A lizard lounging on a flat rock gives me an appraising stare. I stare back.

The path to the river is hot in the morning sun, but before long, running water and birdsong reach my ears, and then the grass turns silky, softening my steps.

The riverbanks are full of people, some lounging about, some singing, others playing games of dice. One woman rests on her back with her eyes closed, humming under her breath. So much for my vision of mournful shades wailing in despair!

I stand still for a few minutes, watching, relieved that no one is paying me any attention. But the longer I stand there, the stranger it seems. Everyone is smiling; everyone looks not only happy but ecstatic. It's unreal, like I'm gazing at a scene painted on a vase and the figures are starting to move across the clay.

The sound of splashing makes my feet itch for cool, lapping water. I stroll around a bend, looking for a private spot where I can wade in alone. In a few minutes I come to a curve in the bank where a pale-leafed tree stands guard, and I pause, listening.

I still hear singing, but it's no longer drifting over from the shades. No, the song seems to rise from the river itself. It ripples through me until I'm swaying to its rhythm. My feet start dancing a graceful grapevine toward the water, and as I dance, the morning's worries lift off my shoulders. Hades' disappearance, getting lost in the castle, my total ignorance about how to play queen—the river's music is carrying it all away. I'm humming, then singing along to a gentle, alluring song whose words I somehow know.

I lift my chiton above my knees, ready to wade in, when a faint shout interrupts the music. I shake my head like a horse trying to get rid of an annoying fly, but the harsh noise comes again and again. I look up, irritated. There's a rider galloping from the palace, waving a hand frantically overhead.

My toes wiggle deeper into the grass. I raise my chiton

another inch as the black horse devours the ground with its hooves and the rider's cloak streams out behind him.

It's Hades.

Hades! A burst of pleasure fills me—look how fast he's rushing to reach me! His tenderness last night suffuses my body again, and I melt. I'll wait for him. We'll go for a swim together, and then he'll explain why he wasn't by my side when I woke.

He gallops up, leaps from the horse's sweating back, and pulls me roughly aside.

"Not that river!" he says, his voice raspy. "Anywhere but there." He's holding my arm too hard. It hurts. "By Cerberus, it's good I came when I did."

That's not what I expected to hear. Where's the apology? The kiss? So I answer sharply, "It's good you came when you did? It's good you abandoned me to wake up all alone? I didn't even know there'd be sun! I thought there'd be moaning wraiths everywhere!"

"I've been away so much, I had business to attend to." He lets go of my arm so he can put both hands on my shoulders. "How was I to know you rise before the birds? I came back to wake you and you were gone. And the way jewels and clothing were scattered around, it looked like thieves had snatched you away."

His anxious voice, his creased brow . . . "You were worried!" I exclaim. "You!"

Because of me.

I kiss him, not caring who sees. But the shades keep humming and playing on the banks, oblivious.

Finally Hades says, "Come." He leads me to the tree and we sit under its leafy branches. He wraps an arm around my shoulders. I lean into his side, and when he speaks, I feel his voice vibrating in his chest.

"When I came back to our room this morning, I was looking forward to waking you myself. And then, actually, I planned to bring you here. To show you your new home's beauties. And its dangers."

He looks pointedly at the river. It flows just as gently and innocuously as before.

I snort. "Dangers! It's not exactly a raging torrent. And it's already full of people. If the river's so dangerous, why aren't you trying to save *them*?"

"Because they're the reason it's here," he says, shifting back against the trunk and holding me tighter. "You see, some shades like thinking about their life on Earth, but for many, memory is an enemy. They grouse about what they left behind—wrongs done them, and tasks left unfinished. They wail about children in danger. They pick fights. In short, they're miserable. And that makes trouble. For them, there's the Lethe. The River of Forgetting."

Across the distance, laughter rises and floats away like steam.

Hades looks at me. "Don't you hear the river calling?"

"But it's so joyous, so peaceful! It couldn't do any harm."

He shakes his head. "Those who accept the river's embrace lose their pain, but they also lose their past, their memories, their very names. They're happy precisely because they forget who they were."

"Can't they go in just a little bit, maybe dip in a toe, and ease their pain without losing themselves?"

"In theory," he says. "But the Lethe is a powerful drug. Once touched, it's too delicious to resist in full."

I try to listen more closely. Now the water's enticing song seems to be made of a thousand twining notes. It's as if each drop of water were a voice surrendered to the river.

"But they're shades, Hades. It might not do the same to me."

"Why risk losing everything for the sake of an experiment?" he says. "What if those beautiful eyes of yours were blank? Your body nothing but an empty shell? That's not what I want sharing my bed." I cuddle closer as he reaches his other arm around and runs a warm hand slowly along my arm.

Then, in a more practical voice, he adds, "Or ruling beside me. What if the Lethe swallowed your power?"

"Me? Power?" I have to laugh. "I don't know why you keep saying that."

"I want you for you. All of you." He stands and gives me his hand. "Now let me show you around."

He lifts me onto the horse and leaps up behind me. With an arm firmly circling my waist, he nuzzles my neck and nudges the horse on with his heels.

We ride past a gleaming temple, open to the skies and guarded by ghostly white poplars. A golden throne with lion legs gleams on a white marble dais. Hades' voice murmurs in my ear. "For outdoor festivals."

We ride and ride and ride along a wall that's taller than two horses. "Our borders have never been broached," he says with pride. "These walls circle our realm, except where rivers do the job. You've seen the Lethe. Now I'll show you the Phlegethon, if you're not bored yet."

Bored? My eyes are more open than they've ever been, drinking up a brand-new world. The warm, dusty air smells like perfume to me. The horse's hooves make music as Hades holds me close.

At one point he gestures to a gate where the sun enters each morning, crossing our lands when it's night on Earth. So *that's* why the sun is here. There are other gates, too, all firmly closed, and yet the walls feel as comfortable as Hades' arm, like a golden ring on a willing finger.

I smell sulfur and a smoky scent like burning torches. We round a bend and look down a cliff and I cry, "The river's on fire!"

"It isn't *on* fire," says Hades. "It *is* fire. Pure flame flows through the Phlegethon's banks, charring them black. That bronze door on the other side is the entrance to Tartarus."

Tartarus, prison for Titans and miscreant gods. In spite of the heat, I shiver, and Hades turns the horse around. "Don't worry," he says. "They can't escape, any more than mortal shades can cross back over the River Styx."

"Show me," I say. Anything to stay like this, wrapped in Hades' arm.

The horse's rhythmic step lulls me, and I lose track of time. Finally we stop, and Hades points to a curving road that disappears into thick trees.

"The Styx is over there. That river won't burn you, or suck out your identity, but don't try to go wading across. It has its own dangers. The banks are ferociously guarded."

"Guarded against what?"

"Escape. Charon the ferryman brings shades across that border from Zeus's realm, but no one crosses in the other direction. No one. Cerberus makes sure of that."

"Let's go see it."

"We'll have to do it another day." He glances up at the sun. "We took longer than I expected. Now it's time to prepare for your grand entrance."

"My *what?*"

"Today you enter the throne room as my queen."

I don't say anything the whole ride back to the palace, and I barely see the land around me. I think there are more streams, and we go through a gate, but I'm not sure. I'm too busy worrying.

I Take My Throne

Servant girls bathe me in the red marble bathtub. They anoint my skin with rose-scented oil until I glisten. They drape me in a purple chiton with golden, three-headed dogs guarding the hem. Gingerly, they fix in glittering brooches and place a broad girdle around my waist. They bend obsequiously, strapping my feet in ruby-studded sandals. Without a word, they hold out earrings for my approval: intricate golden boats, a small oarsman in the center of each, and delicate diamond stars dangling from bow and stern. When I nod, the servants slip them in my ears and the stars tickle my shoulders. They load heavy bracelets on my wrists and drape yokes of jewels around my neck. After spending ages on my tangled locks, they hold up a mirror to show me rubies glittering like fire in the dark night of my elegant hair. Then comes my crown: a blazing circlet of golden leaves. Finally, kneeling before me, they bow their obeisance, signaling that they're done.

At the door, another servant meekly bobs her head then turns to show me the way. I guess we're not taking any chances I'll get lost. It's time for my grand entrance. I'm about to take my throne.

My stomach rises in my throat.

I thought about the ceremony the whole time they were dressing me, and I've decided how to get through it. I'll enter quietly and make my way discreetly to the dais. Then I'll put my feet on the little footstool like I've seen in pictures, and I'll sit tall and keep my mouth shut. I won't do or say a thing. I'll just watch and listen. That way, nothing can go wrong. I'll be like a silent sponge on the ocean floor, letting the water waft information through my open pores.

My golden sandals clatter down the corridor, echoing into rooms as we pass. It's not like the early morning when the halls were deserted; servants are everywhere, and they're all kneeling on the floor with lowered heads. I want to grab their hands and pull them up, but I don't.

We come to the stairway where the statue of Hades and the three-headed dog stand guard. But once we go down the stairs we turn right, down a new hall. I peer in at the doors to either side as we pass. Another room full of vases. Another lined with wooden boxes. Another—and then I stop.

In a light, spacious room looking out on a courtyard, a loom stands fully threaded. Silver weights pull the warp threads straight and true, just begging for the shuttle. A silver basket bubbles with balls of yarn. I step closer. There, carved at the top of the loom, is my name: *Persephone*.

"My lady!" says the servant girl in a tiny, frightened voice. "My lady, forgive me, but we'll be late!"

I pull myself away from the loom and follow her into the grandest hallway yet. A double row of broad red pillars leads to a wall with stone blocks the size of sheep, and gigantic double doors. We pause in front of the thick wooden panels, and I can hear rustling and the muted hum of voices.

I'm breathing so hard the girdle feels tight around my waist, and the heavy necklaces rise and fall on my chest like boats riding the waves.

I can do this. I throw back my shoulders and try to stand tall like a tree stretching toward the sun. Taking a deep breath, I nod. The servant girl throws open the doors and stands back for me to pass.

A hush falls over the cavernous room. Somewhere up in the ether, a roof disappears above red columns. Waves of cloaks and chitons rustle as a sea of faces turns my way. At the far end of all those bodies, Hades rises from a benchlike throne big enough for two. Now he stands, waiting for me.

Even from this distance, his hair is burnished blacker against golden robes. Where is the man I fell in love with, the one with an easy smile, the one lounging next to me on the grass? The man in front of me now is pure power, a god-king.

And me?

I realize everyone is staring at me: my dress, my jewels, my hands, my hair, my face. I take a step and people move back, creating a path.

Only the *click, click* of my sandals breaks the terrible silence. Left foot, right foot, head high, left foot, shoulders back, right foot—right foot! My sandal lands on a long cloak. Its owner, gasping in apology, jerks it away—and my right foot with it. The slippery gold sole flies out behind me as my arms grab at the air. I'm suspended. Time stops. Just me in midair screeching and every single eye glued to me as I crash to the floor, my bracelets clattering like a handful of coins flung on a table.

A winged man picks up my crown, then holds out his other hand to help me up. I take it and come to my feet. My face feels so hot, I must be blushing as red as the rubies in my hair.

Don't even ask me about the rest of it. The man hands me my crown. He's smiling. Everyone in the whole damn room is probably smiling, trying to swallow their snickers.

Somehow I make my way up to the throne. Hades takes my hand and squeezes it as we face the sea of faces together. He doesn't let go. He probably thinks he has to hold me up so I won't fall over again.

I sit and he sits and then an eternity passes. People approach and lay gifts before us. I clutch the arm of the throne so tightly, the three-headed dog carved into the gold bites my hand. People talk and Hades responds, and I don't hear a single word they're saying. So much for being a sponge.

Cocoon

My covers weigh me down like a shroud. But the outer world keeps insisting on its existence: I can hear carts clanking outside, and servants bustling somewhere down the hall. I pull the covers over my head. Why does the world of death have to be so damn purposeful? I wish I could rot in peace.

It's no good. I'm going to have to get up and face it. Them. Everyone who saw me yesterday making my—what was it Hades called it?—my "grand entrance."

I told him, didn't I? I told him back in the vale that I wasn't queen material, and he looked right into my eyes and said it didn't matter. *Ruling is easy*, he said. *I'll teach you*, he said.

And then he throws me into the throne room like a fish to sharks.

Now he can see what kind of queen he brought home. Not someone dignified and regal like my mother; no, he's got a bumbling girl who can't even walk a simple path. Some immortal I am!

I groan out loud. Queen Persephone the Hilarious, that's me. I can see it now. Everyone will smile politely when I pass, then turn to each other, whispering and covering their mouths to stifle their giggles. Oh, this is going to be just great.

I sit up in the dark, gathering my covers into a huge, padded cocoon with only my face and feet poking out. I shuffle over and open the shutters. Then I plop back down on the bed and look around.

Grand. Elegant. Imposing. Queenly. Nothing at all like me. Nothing like home.

I wriggle out of my cocoon. As I reach for a chiton, I realize I'm humming. What is that tune? I can't quite place it . . . something about green grass and water and—I stop cold. Of course! It's the Lethe's song.

The Lethe, River of Forgetting. Put in a toe and you might forget what you had for breakfast. Put in your leg up to the knee and there go your weaving patterns. But step in all the way, dunk your head under, and you come out dripping, sleek, sopping, and gone.

I hum a little more. That doesn't sound so bad right now: forgetting. Maybe I could wade in just a little, up to my ankles, and make yesterday go away.

But as I fasten a girdle around my waist, waves of pictures sweep over me, and I realize there's so much I don't want to forget. Hades' hands lifting me into the chariot. And my friends—maybe the only friends I'll ever have, since everyone here is too busy bowing at my feet to get to know me. And the vale: dark green leaves on gnarled branches, purple drifts of irises by the lake, my courtyard (how small it was!), and the lemon tree near the overhang shading my loom . . .

That's it! The loom I passed yesterday on my way to the throne: it's already strung and waiting just for me. My name is carved on it, after all, and that silver yarn basket isn't something a servant would use.

My mother never taught me to rule, but she did make me weave for so many hours, my hands take over and I don't need to think, or analyze, or worry as long as the shuttle is moving.

It's too bad the Lethe can't be measured out to my liking. As it is, I'm stuck being me, no matter how much I mess up, and I might as well figure out how to make this my home. I'll start by weaving some new covers for this bed, something with a cheerful pattern, not so regal.

I tie my hair back and throw open the door.

Statues

The hallways rear up like a hydra waving serpentine heads. I've already forgotten my path from yesterday morning.

What's more, all the servants I heard bustling about earlier have disappeared, leaving me alone with a jumble of rooms and hallways. Against all the spirals and frescoes, the only figures I can see are statues, stiff with perfection. Every corner seems to shelter someone brandishing a sword or stepping from a chariot.

Then it occurs to me—the doorways all look the same, but each statue has some distinguishing characteristic. I'll use them to keep track of where I've been, and eventually, when I have a map in my head, I'll find my way downstairs.

A fellow with a traveler's hat and winged sandals must be Hermes. He raises his staff, preparing to guide mortal spirits away from their earthly bodies. What a handsome face he has: boyish and a little playful.

I walk down the hall toward a towering statue of Hades, confident, bold, and totally regal. In fact, there are statues of Hades just about everywhere. Hades, reins in hand, leading eight horses across a frieze. Hades in a gesture of welcome, standing near a staircase.

These may not be the stairs I took yesterday, but they go down, don't they?

With every step I hear a rhythmic tapping. The lower I go, the louder the sound gets until it saturates the air around me. Where there's banging, there's bound to be a person to ask for directions.

I follow the noise through a door into a courtyard, except it's like I've walked into a cloud, because white dust is swirling everywhere. Craggy shapes loom up like stones scattered on a hillside in the mist. I cover my mouth with my hand and try to wend my way toward the banging noise.

I round one of the rocks and suddenly a gigantic shoulder is writhing toward me out of the stone. I lurch back, preparing to flee; then I realize the muscled, surging shoulder is nothing but marble. A statue in the making, that's what it is.

As I come among more finished work, I start to recognize some of the statues. Right in front of me there's a white marble man with wings raised above broad shoulders. Even though the stone isn't painted yet, his face looks familiar, and so do the greaves etched on muscular calves. Then I remember a smile on that face, and those wings folded back, and that hand helping me up from the throne room floor.

Now the hammering is almost deafening. I can see an arm going up and down just past a curving backside, the only statue of a woman in this whole place. I walk carefully through the cloud enveloping her, and there's the crafts-man, chiseling away in a controlled frenzy. He must be close to done, because his creation is already laden with bracelets and necklaces. Her hair is perfectly coifed, without a single loose tendril. Slender and graceful, she stands regally with an ease I envy.

The sculptor steps back and gives the face an appraising look. I follow his gaze to the statue's strong chin, her generous mouth, her eyes—the eyes I see in my mirror every morning.

I freeze as still as the stone. Even my breath stops.

It's me.

Except the statue of me looks like she actually knows what she's doing. I try to mimic her perfect posture, her noble expression, the set of her mouth—but then the dust tickles my nose and I explode with a gigantic, most un-regal sneeze. The sculptor looks my way, smiles, and wipes his hands on his dust-coated tunic.

"Excuse me," I say. "I'm trying to find the weaving room."

His look goes as blank as an untouched slab of rock. Without my throne and jewels I must be invisible, even though he's just been carving my face.

"You know, where the loom is set up? I can't seem to find my way around."

He shakes his head. "Not my business, weaving."

Then I remember the statue of Hades with his hand on Cerberus's head. I describe it, and the sculptor lights up.

"That's one of mine!" he says, leading me back to the door. He points toward yet another corridor. "Through there, miss," he says, "and then a sharp left will take you where you're going."

The warp strings stand at attention, held taut by their silver weights. I roll the gleaming basket closer on its little wheels and rummage through the balls of yarn. A soft greeny brown settles in my hand. Soon the boxwood shuttle starts its dance. My hand follows in its wake, and before long I drift into a place close to dreaming.

I feel like myself again. Something more than the infamous tripping queen.

That statue in the courtyard knows more about ruling than I do. They should tote her up to the throne room whenever they need a figurehead. She'd accept their homage without fluttering an eyelash, content to be nothing but a symbol, a receptacle for their prayers. She'd probably even look more at home in the fancy clothes.

She's got it easy. She doesn't have a heart to hammer so loud she can't think.

I pick up a richer brown now and wind it on the shuttle.

Look at me! I don't belong on that throne. I'm only here because I happened to fall in love. I don't have a clue what shades want—or what they need. What, exactly, does a queen do?

The dark brown makes wavy lines, like branches.

Let's take an inventory of my skills, shall we? I'm good with friends, and plants, and weaving. That's hardly enough to justify a crown.

The shuttle meanders, pulling the brown lines wider.

And I don't even have any friends here, let alone a blossoming vale. There's only this loom. So I'll have to make weaving be enough. This and Hades' strong arms should be enough to make my life here work. Right?

But even as I try to convince myself, my hand tightens on the shuttle and my foot itches to kick the silver basket across the room.

A tight hand makes tight weaving, my mother always said, and the bit of cloth I've just woven is as puckered as pinched lips. I pull out the offending strands, then gaze at the picture on my loom. The brown needs something brighter for balance.

I grab a bursting green and start plucking bits of color like bright notes across the fabric. Then I wrap them with a deeper green, rounding the edges into curves until they're unfurling like new leaves.

All right, that's what they'll be: bright life sprouting from soft, woolen earth. More color now. I'll jumble some blossoms in among the leaves, so it looks like spring branches when everything is illuminated from the inside. I pick up a dark purple, but it's a late-summer color, like ripe plums pulling a branch low or juicy grapes crowding on the vine.

I toss the purple back in the basket and start pacing.

The only garden I have now is on my loom. No fresh water cascading over rocks to cool my fingers, no rich-smelling soil, no leaves as soft as lambs' ears. Just wool.

What I'd give for a garden of my own, here, in the underworld!

Then the loom seems to whisper, *"Why don't you?"*

Oh, right, trash my image even more. Who ever heard of a queen digging in the dirt, coming home with a mud-streaked chiton? I've probably done enough damage already, waltzing around barefoot.

"Why don't you?"

Because queens are dignified, that's why. I'm not a country girl anymore. I have a household to learn to run, a position to uphold, responsibility to exercise . . . if I can ever figure out what I'm supposed to do.

The shuttle, having wormed its way back into my hand, is making the fat purple grapes.

I think of my mother walking barefoot out of the court-yard, her hand already reaching to caress a glistening lemon leaf.

"Why don't you?"

Just a little garden. I'll put it near that big oak where the hill flattens out, halfway between the palace and the Lethe's plain. It's not like I'm going to wave my hands and shout, "Hey, look, everyone! Here's a queen digging around in the dirt!" No, I'll work there quietly, and the moist soil will root me and the warmth of sun-soaked leaves will revive me, and I'll be me again.

Roots

Out past the stables, where the land is rough and rocky, my fingers run along sturdy leaves. They're as pointy and determined as miniature swords. I stop to scratch my nose, and an astringent scent clears my head, so everything looks crisper.

Rosemary.

It's a small bush, a baby, with four woody shoots reaching straight up. I'll carry it back to the oak, the first transplant for my new garden.

I pull a spade from my girdle. The ridiculous tool is gold, with chunky jewels protruding all over. It's hard to get anything practical at the palace unless you're very, very specific.

Everyone assumes a queen wants only luxurious fabrics, the most exotic perfumes, the rarest unguents. Do they really expect me to walk around in the diamond-encrusted sandals they keep giving me, with huge earrings pulling down my earlobes and golden chains clanking all over my neck? So when I asked for a spade, I should have known better. Tonight I'll tell them to make me one from solid iron, unembellished. But for now this will have to do.

The gold bends the second it encounters a stone, and when I grip harder, the faceted gems dig into my palm. But the soil is fairly loose, and between the feeble blade and some good old-fashioned scrabbling with my hands, I dig down around the roots. They're young and resilient, like the rest of the plant. Finally they're free, and I cradle the plant in one arm while I stick the so-called spade back in my girdle. Maybe they can melt the gold down and use it for something else.

As I walk back toward the palace, warmth seems to flow out from the little bush, surrounding me in a kind of expanding lightness. It floats me along so I barely feel like I'm touching the ground.

Now I see dust rising near the stables, and even from here I can make out a rider astride a rearing horse. The man's body has such strength and confidence, I know it must be Hades. Of course! It's the new stallion he was telling me about. He wouldn't trust a groom to break it in; he wants that horse to know his hands, his scent, his voice.

I angle off toward the stables, eager to watch him at his work. I lean against the fence rail.

The stallion is panicky, snorting and tossing its huge head, but Hades' hands are easy on the reins and his face is alive with concentration, reading every message the horse sends with its snorts and whinnies, the angle of its ears, the muscles tensing in its flanks.

Suddenly, the horse leaps off the ground and takes to the air. I shake my head—it shouldn't be possible! This is a smooth-backed riding horse, not a winged horse for the chariot. When I get my breath back, I look at Hades' face. He's laughing in sheer pleasure.

Then he catches sight of me and says something into the horse's ear. The great beast circles and lands, as tame as a house cat after its amazing feat. Hades jumps off, murmurs something low and soothing, then waves to a groom, who runs up and takes the reins.

Hades strolls over and leans on the other side of the fence from me, all sweaty and exhilarated.

"Isn't he a beauty?" he says. "And now you're here. I seem to be surrounded by beauty today."

He runs a finger across my cheek, making me shiver with his energy. He's leaning in closer when he notices the gangly little plant trapped between us. He pauses, lifting one eyebrow in an inquiring way.

"What are you up to? Taking up cooking?"

I'm still too befuddled by the feel of his hand to answer. So he goes on. "Ah. I see you've got the roots, too. Why?"

"So I can plant it," I say, finding my voice. "I'm making a garden."

Now the second eyebrow goes up to join the first one.

"A garden? Where, near the palace?"

"I need it there, Hades. We need it. The building is full of pillars and frescoes, but no one ever bothered about what's right outside the walls. Look at this!"

He follows my gaze.

"Just scraggly, dry grass and rambly weeds," I say. "Why? It isn't that plants won't grow here. This rosemary's healthy enough, and the riverbanks are crowded with bushes." I smile, teasing him now. "No, it's plain laziness on your part."

He gets the strangest look, almost like a child staring at a plate of cakes, eager to reach out and grab one.

"Where will you put it?" he asks.

"Near that oak tree halfway down the hill, where it flattens out. There's an easy path from the palace forecourt, and I can use the little stream that runs nearby for a fountain. There are lots of young trees near the Lethe; I'll dig up a small one. Maybe I can even find berry bushes or some mossy rocks for the stream."

He's hardly listening. He reaches up to run his fingers

along one of the rosemary's spiky little swords.

"A green garden near the palace. Perfect," he says. His voice is almost dreamy.

Then he catches himself, shakes his head, and some kind of shutters come down over his eyes. When they come up again, he's all practical.

"I'll call workers to prepare the soil for you. They can get started on that fountain."

"I want to do it myself, Hades."

He gives me that strange smile again. "So it will be all yours!"

"So I can listen to what it wants to be."

As soon as I get myself a decent spade.

As I walk up the hill, I can't stop thinking about that eager look on Hades' face. I suppose he just wants me to be happy here. After all, he wouldn't do any gardening himself. He practically ran back to his new horse, those broad hands itching for reins, not a trowel. And he didn't offer to come but to send workmen. Workmen? I want to prepare the soil with my own hands. And it would feel funny to do this with strangers.

Now, if my friends were here, that would be different. Kallirhoe would show me where to place rocks for the stream, and Admete—Admete never did a purposeful day's work in her life, but she'd brighten everything with her laughter. Ianthe could tell me what each flower likes best, and Galaxaura would waft, calm and clear, among the bushes, cooling us down as we worked.

Between us, we'd have water running and paths curving in no time. And a riot of leaves would spring up, dark green and yellow-green and gray-green. We'd search for golden crocuses and orange-red poppies and bring them back to brighten the foliage, like stars across the sky.

I reach the oak and walk under its leafy branches, leaning against the trunk in heavy shade. A breeze rustles the leaves, sighing low and sad. Then the sigh is mine.

Kallirhoe, Ianthe, Galaxaura—I gave you up to come here. And Admete, already gone. I miss you all. I miss your voices, the way you know me through and through.

What did you think when I didn't come back?

The wind shifts the leaves, deepening the darkness around me. Outside the circle of branches, the sun blinds the world into nothing but glare.

They don't know where I am. I never told them.

How did they learn I'd left the vale? Maybe it was my mother. I can almost see her striding down to the lake, her lips taut with anger, storm clouds billowing over the cliffs. I see her interrogating my friends, and when they try to say they don't know where I am, her face winches tighter—

Enough! The oak's deep shade must be making me moody.

I blink my way out from under the branches so the light can burnish my doubts away. I pull out the feeble spade and start digging a hole, pushing the dark down deeper, where I don't have to look at it.

What am I worrying about? Everyone must know where I am by now. I'm sure someone saw me flying overhead in the chariot, and the gods gossip together all the time. Besides, my mother, care that I'm gone? Enough to be that angry? I don't think so. Oh, she felt obligated to instruct me and improve me, but I don't think she liked me very much.

I swallow, trying to get rid of a bitter taste in my mouth. Then I plop the rosemary in its new home and scoop the soil back around its roots.

Queen Lessons

"Shorter steps," he says. "You don't want to look like you're rushing."

Hades is sitting on the edge of the bed, leaning back a bit, his hands on the covers behind him. I take a few jerky steps, and the crown slips over my eyes.

"That's one way to do it," he says, laughing. I wind my loose hair up into a knot and shove the crown back on. Better. I go back to my starting point across the room.

"Again," he says. "Shoulders back, easy stride, a look of confidence."

I take a few steps and then stumble again.

"It's these stupid shoes!" I cry, leaning down and yanking

them off. I throw them at him and he catches one.

"Look at them," I tell him. "Solid gold soles!"

"Distinctly opulent," he says. "Nothing but the finest."

"Opulent or not, they're too slippery. That's why I can't walk. I need new shoes."

"Practice barefoot for now," he says. "All the way to the throne this time and then turn to face the audience. Sit down slowly, your back straight. If you hold the arm of the throne, it's easier to do without looking."

"Where's the throne?"

He sits upright at the edge of the bed, legs together, elbows bent into the arms of a chair. "My lady, your throne awaits."

I try to put on a regal expression as I walk over with neat, precise steps. I stop in front of him, turn to face the door, put my hands on his forearms, and my back ever so straight, slowly sit down.

The arms of the throne wrap around me. "Very well done," it says in a most unthronelike voice.

"Let's do it again."

The throne sighs and releases its hold. I walk back to my starting point, adjust the crown again, take a step, and stop.

"Hades," I say, thinking. "This is all show."

He shrugs. "Perhaps, but show is important. It's half the work."

"That's just it." I take off the crown and walk back to him in my normal walk. "What's the other half? Other than sit upright and look pretty, what does a queen do?"

I plop down beside him on the covers.

"Greet shades in the throne room, of course." He relaxes back on his hands again. "Make them feel welcome. In time you'll grow more comfortable speaking in front of crowds, and then you can help with the explanations if you like."

"Is that all?"

"You can run the palace any way you please. I've never entertained much, but if you like that kind of thing, go ahead. And ladies like to weave, don't they?"

Something is missing. "Shouldn't I do more than that?"

He tilts his head to the side, looking thoughtful. "You could help shades settle their conflicts, I suppose. I don't enjoy it so I tend to send them off to the Lethe. If you took over, I'd have more time for other things. Borders. Inventory." He smiles. "Horses."

I twiddle the crown around and around in sparkling circles. Hades looks from my hands to my face.

"Look," he says more seriously. "There isn't one way to be a queen, any more than there's one way to be a woman."

"You said you'd teach me!"

"But you want more than I can teach, so you'll have to sort it out yourself. Having you by my side in the throne room and the mere fact that you're here—that's enough for me. If you want to do more, figure it out and take it on."

"Damn," I say. "That's harder."

"Then let's work on the easy part first." He bends his arms back into armrests and looks at me with a rakish smile. "How about a little more throne practice?"

The River Styx

My fountain is running beautifully, the water cascading into a narrow streambed. Chamomile and thyme are already creeping eager fingers across the soil, but I need something with more height here, like river reeds. There aren't any by the Lethe, with all its silky green grass, and anyway I can't go wading in there. It's time I explored the River Styx.

I toss my new trowel into a collecting bag and head toward the low hills. Before long I'm at the top of the curving road, where the trees cluster in copses and I can hear the river. Its song is so different from the Lethe's: low-voiced, like thick, dark strands of thread twisted together. A rope for hangings.

A few more steps and I can see the river and its pebbled shore. The banks are crowded with reeds, some knee-high, others stretching above my shoulders. Swamp irises tangle among them and vines tendril in and out among the stalks. It will be good collecting here.

I pull my chiton up to my knees and wade a few inches into the wide river. Cool water tingles my skin, and there's a strong, remorseless current. I don't see any animals around. This isn't a river that would pause to reunite a stray duckling with its mother, or even wait for me to regain my footing if I slipped. I'd better watch my step.

I look up the pebbly shore. Something's peeking out from a clump of bushes. I walk closer and find a boat pulled up on land, oars tucked neatly along the sides. Someone's kept her paint in good trim, cleaned the hull, fixed and filled her scrapes.

It reminds me of the boat back home, and how we'd slip the rope off the trunk where she was tied, push her toward the middle of the glassy lake, and lie flat in the bottom. We'd float like that, not even steering, drifting wherever the water wanted us to go. On our backs we were part of the wood, the water, and the clouds overhead.

I wouldn't mind feeling like that again. Even though the sturdy little boat is on land and not gently rocking water, I climb in and lie on my back, staring at the sky.

I watch the clouds for a while—ten minutes? twenty?—

and then I hear an old man's voice rasping out a raucous tune. I don't want him to see me. I try to flatten myself down so I'm invisible, but the voice gets louder and pebbles crunch closer, and suddenly a gnarled, ruddy face is leaning right over the edge of the boat. Bushy eyebrows hoist up like a sail, disappearing under a woolen cap, and hands like old leather freeze in midair, leaving a bag suspended.

"What the—" A strong scent of ouzo wafts my way. "And just what do you think you're doin' in my boat, girl?"

I sit up guiltily.

"A man goes off for a little drink and a quick toss of the dice, and look what happens. You're lucky my four-legged partner's across the river right now, that's all I can say."

He's gruff, but I don't think there's any bite in him. So I venture to say, "It's a very nice boat."

"Aye, she's a beauty." His hand caresses the gunnels as if they were silk.

I give him my best smile. "Is there any chance you'd take me for a row?"

"Listen here, girl. I can't take you nowhere. Look at you, all smilin' and innocent-like. You know as good as I do, I only take 'em in one direction."

The Styx, a sailor's cap . . . Suddenly I remember my earrings with the ferryman and the boat dangling stars into the currents of time.

"Oh, you mean you're—"

He nods. "Aye. Charon at your service. Or not at your service, if you get my drift. I only take people in one direction. If you're on this shore, this here is where you're stayin'.'"

What luck! Charon is the first one shades see when they arrive in the underworld. He can help me.

Here's the thing. I've been back to the throne room a number of times now. I haven't tripped again, and the last time, I was even calm enough to hear myself think. But that's the part Hades himself calls "show." For the other part, the half Hades says I have to figure out for myself, I need to know more about mortals. And here I am dressed like one of them, so Charon is talking free and easy.

I wish I had some ouzo to pour out and keep his words flowing. Instead I say, "I'd love to hear more, Charon. It must be very hard, what you do."

"No, it's fine work," he says with a shake of his head. He points to the far bank. "I start out over there and the shades climb on all slouched-like, just starin' at the ground, shufflin' like there's no energy left in 'em at all. Like slaves taken in battle and shoved into the victor's boat, that's how they look, like everything they'll ever love is back behind 'em. I used to smile, tell a few jokes, but it never made no difference. So now I let 'em be. Help 'em into the boat, show 'em where to sit. While I'm rowin' across, they start to sit a little lighter. Not that they say anything, not that they ever smile or laugh, but it's like the heaviness in 'em starts to let go."

He takes off his hat and scratches some thin gray curls.

"You know how a sleepin' baby weighs like a lump in your arms, but then it wakes and holds up its own head and all of a sudden it's lighter? It's like that in my boat. There's less weight in their shoulders. The water helps 'em let go."

"Still, you're at the oars all day, and every day, too. Death never takes a break, does he?"

"And it's been busier than usual lately, too. Some kind of drought up there, I hear. But still, I don't mind rowin'; I like it. Done it so many years now, my arms know the rhythm. They need it. You pull against the water and the water resists you. So you convince it you're gonna go, and it hears your oars, lets you go easy. I think on that, my oars in the water. I let them shades be."

He finally puts his bundle down in the boat. "Well, looky here." He pulls up a coin and tosses it over his shoulder. It lands with a clink on a mountain of identical coins piled farther up the shore. "Still don't know why they think I need these."

He reaches out a craggy hand, pulls me up, and helps me over the side of the boat. "I found out a long time ago, I can't make no difference to 'em. Got to trust the water to do that. I just give 'em a hand out on this shore. Lately I've been rowin' back and forth all day. Bring one over; take back the empty boat for the next one. My boat practically flies back when it's only her and me."

He starts to push the boat back into the water. The hull scrapes across pebbles, underlining his voice like untuned lyre strings.

"But I just brought one over a little while ago, and see over there, across on that bank? No one waitin'. So then I get a little break. I round up my friends, share a few, have a laugh. Then I come back to my darlin'."

He pats the side of the boat, then hops in lightly and sits at the oars. "But no one ever rides back over with me. Ever. It don't matter who you are, or who you were, back there: king, queen, war hero, best athlete. Sometimes women beg because a brand-new baby's back on the other side. It don't matter. No one goes from this shore to that one except me and my dogs. I don't care how pretty your smile is or who you got to see or what you got to do. Once you're here, girl, you're here."

He says good-bye with a nod and a wink. He's already digging his oars into the water and pulling away.

I turn back toward the reeds. As I open my collecting bag, I'm surprised by a twinge of sadness. No one goes back across, no one. That goes for immortals, too.

Oh, I don't regret coming. I'd make the same choice all over again. It's the never going back that's just a little hard.

The Sapling

Thanatos brings me a just-awakening sapling of a lemon tree.

"Here," he says, "I think you dropped this."

"Very funny."

He never lets me forget the time I tripped on my way to the throne, when he helped me up and handed me my crown. It's an old joke now.

He grins, pleased with himself, and the stark planes of his face burst into light. He's a handsome fellow. His muscled shoulders shine almost as brightly as his breastplate, and the legs under his short tunic are strong, like those of a warrior back from months on the march. That's not why the calves behind those bronze greaves are so shapely, though. After all, he flies everywhere. Wings like an eagle's fold gracefully behind him.

"Do you like it?" he asks.

"I love it. It's lucky for me you get to travel between the worlds. And that you're so thoughtful."

Thanatos. His name means death. Mortals know all about him, how he frees the soul birds to fly from their earthly bodies and introduces them to Hermes, their guide to Charon's boat. But do they know what a handsome man he is, or how eager to be helpful?

Come to think of it, they probably wish he were a little less helpful.

He gazes approvingly at my garden, now densely carpeted with thyme and chamomile. The fountain burbles in the center, spilling water onto mossy rocks, and reeds sprout from a small pool.

"Isn't it time you took a rest, Persephone? You're always working out here in the garden."

"This isn't work. This is my idea of fun."

"All right. Just so you don't go collapsing from exhaustion," he says. "Wouldn't want to have to pick you up."

"Ha-ha."

He grins and turns, raising a hand in farewell.

"And Thanatos—thank you."

"It's entirely my pleasure."

His easy stride swallows up the path to the castle. He's probably on his way to give Hades another report about conditions on Earth. Apparently it's a very dry season and harvests are so scanty, people don't have enough to eat. There's more sickness, even starvation. When I first came, I was in the throne room once a week, dressed in an elaborate chiton with the jeweled crown perched on my head. Now it's twice as often, and so many shades are coming, they pack the room from wall to wall.

The weird thing is that Hades doesn't seem tired by the extra work, or cross to be called away from his horses. He actually seems invigorated by the hordes of new arrivals. I try to follow his lead, but there's a part of me that keeps getting stuck. Maybe it's because I know what it's like to leave something behind forever. Every time I look out over the throne room, I think, each one of these shades misses someone, and is missed in return.

I hope the dry season ends soon.

I look at my rosemary bush; it's already waist-high. When I first got here, it never occurred to me that the underworld could be greener than Earth. But my garden is thriving. Everything I plant seems to sprout and spread the instant I put it in new soil.

I worried for a while that I was being selfish, making this as a refuge for myself, some kind of greedy pleasure. But then I realized the garden isn't just for me. It helps everyone in the underworld. I've put a bench in a private little spot near lavender bushes. Shades come wandering over and sit, resting. I can see the pleasure on their faces and how relaxation softens their shoulders. They find peace in my garden, without having to lose themselves in the Lethe. It's good for them.

And it's good for me, too. You see, people only realize I'm a queen when I'm wearing my royal regalia, as if they're honoring the trappings themselves: *Hail to the golden bracelets! Bow before the purple chiton!* That's why everyone is so stiff and formal in the throne room. But out here I work quietly in my plainest clothes and people ignore me, talking with each other and saying what's on their minds. I'm finding out a lot about mortals this way.

Like yesterday. I was weeding on the far side of the lavender bushes when an old man pulled a younger man down beside him on the bench.

"Sit," he said, "and tell me what brought you here before your time."

The younger man mumbled something, and the old one shouted, "Speak up! I could have sworn you said something about birds."

"You heard me right!" shouted the young man. I could have been halfway to the palace and still heard him. "Birds!"

He then related the strangest tale. He'd saved a little

grain, he said, and decided to sow it even though the soil was bone dry. But no sooner did he toss out a handful of seeds then crows swooped in and started pecking. Flocks of songbirds fluttered down to join them. Dark clouds appeared on the horizon, and he thought, Rain! But no, it was clouds of seabirds swarming inland. Soon the soil was seething with birds, their claws digging up the dirt, their beaks remorselessly plucking out every last seed.

And birds kept coming. They landed on the plow, and the shed, and then finally all over the young man himself, digging their claws into his flesh. He tried to run; wings blinded him and he tripped, striking his head on the plow.

"That's the wildest story I ever heard!" shouted the old man. "What a way to die! Sounds like you could use a good game of dice to distract you!"

Grasping the young man's arm, he hoisted himself, and they headed downhill toward the green grass, where a lively game was in the works.

So you see? I wouldn't know any of this if it weren't for my garden. Or if I told everyone who I am. The more I hear people's voices, the better I understand them.

I have to wonder about that young man. He must have done something outrageous to anger the gods or why would they punish him in such a bizarre way? All right, not just the gods in general. My mother—because those birds made sure he'd have no harvest. And she always said mortals are like children, needing us to show them right from wrong. I wonder what he did.

The whole thing is making me uncomfortable somehow. I cross my arms, warding off the sensation. It's probably just that I'm thinking about it from down here, and it's a new perspective, so everything looks different. That's all. Like lying on your back and staring at the sky, dizzy with the feeling of falling into the clouds.

I shrug my hands back down and set about planting the sapling. Earth is in other gods' hands. I live here now.

The Traveler

$\mathcal{S}$everal days later, I'm working in my garden when Hades and Hermes come strolling down the path.

They have a good time together, those two. When Hermes is done guiding shades to Charon's boat, he often stops by and lounges with Hades on the golden couches, sipping nectar, and they talk and laugh until all hours. That's how we get most of our news about the other gods on Mount Olympus, and about mortals, too—their heroic feats, or their ill-fated challenges. Gods live forever, after all, and when you live forever, you need novelty to catch your jaded eye. From the way these two talk, mortals are good for that.

So I'm glad to see Hermes. He takes off his broad-brimmed

traveler's hat. His curly hair pops up, and he runs his fingers through it, trying to get it to lie down straight.

He grins at me. "Your garden grows as lovely as its gardener."

Did I mention he's a bit of a flirt?

Hades puts his arm around my shoulder protectively. Doesn't he know he'll never need to worry about me? Other women may cast appreciative glances at Hermes and his winged sandals, but for me there'll never be anyone but Hades. I nestle into his arm.

"It's a relief to see green again," Hermes goes on. "I can't believe you have grapes. Everything is brown up on Earth."

"How bad is the drought?" I ask.

"One of the worst I've seen." Hermes tosses a few grapes in his mouth.

Hades nods. "Charon's been rowing so much, I had to order liniment for his shoulders."

I pull out from under Hades' arm. My hand strays to the vine, but instead of plucking a grape, I start worrying a leaf between my fingers. The unease that I've been trying to ignore suffuses the air around me. Crops failing, birds eating seeds before they can sprout . . .

I lift my head, staring at Hermes. "It's my mother, isn't it?"

Hermes runs his hand through his curls again. "Well, I've heard that—"

"Who knows what the mortals have done this time!" interrupts Hades, staring intently at his friend. "Droughts come and go. They always have and they always will. This is nothing new."

Hermes gives him a strange look. Then his face goes blank.

"You've heard what?" I ask.

"Sorry," says Hermes. "I forgot what I was going to say."

"And it's all my fault!" proclaims Hades, clapping a hand vigorously on his friend's back. "They call me the host with open arms, and here I've forgotten to offer you a drink. Look at you! You're so parched, you're picking the vines clean. I got in some particularly sweet nectar. Let's go back to the palace and I'll pour you some. Persephone, will you join us?"

I shake my head, feeling confused.

Hermes looks at me and shrugs. "You know me, always traveling between one place and another." He smiles an apology as his hand strays back to the vine. "Tell you what, though. Next time I'll bring you some plants or something. Before everything shrivels away on Earth."

He pops another grape, then catches sight of Hades' face. "Just joking! It's bound to rain soon."

Persephones

The day dawns clear. I get dressed as quickly as I can, grab my gardening gear, and head out toward the oak. As I approach, I see someone kneeling in my garden. She's working the earth around some new plantings, pulling out stray strands of grass and loosening clods with her fingers.

I clear my throat, and she jerks her head up like a deer hearing a twig crack. She runs her eyes over the spade in my hand and my simple chiton. A smile illuminates her face.

"Are you the gardener?" she asks. "I was hoping you'd come."

She scrambles to her feet. Her chiton is coarse linen and very plain in style, as if she never had the time to weave a pattern.

She's sturdy looking and brown skinned. Her arms are muscled, and as I come closer, I see her hands are rough. I think she's about my age. A mortal shade, and newly here, I'd guess.

"Is it all right if I work here?" she asks. "This garden is so pretty. Someone's been doing a beautiful job. I bet it's you. You're the one to ask, aren't you?"

I'm tongue-tied. What do I say?

"At home I was always working," she goes on. "I love keeping my hands busy, but here everyone seems to think I should be happy lazing around doing nothing. As if that's fun! I need to work or I'll lose my mind. I bet that's why so many people end up in that river."

She glances toward the Lethe. "I almost went in by mistake. I didn't know it erased you! I was here for days before there were enough of us for the throne room, where they tell you these things. Was it like that for you?"

I'm still frozen. Misinterpreting my silence, she sighs. Her shoulders slump. "I understand. If I'm not supposed to be here, I'll go."

As she starts to walk away, a panicky feeling clutches me: *I'm losing her.*

"No, no!" I call out. "Stay! I *am* the gardener. You're right."

I don't know which is back in front of me faster, her body or her eager smile.

"I, um, I don't know many people here," I say, scrambling for words. "I think I'd like working with you. And I can tell you know your way around plants."

"Really?" She waves a hand toward the palace. "Do I need to clear it with someone official?"

"No. It'll be fine."

She grins, looking ready to burst with energy. Then she sits back down and starts pulling weeds again, chattering away. As I kneel to work beside her, I'm surprised by how light I feel.

She tells me her name is Melita and she comes from a mountain valley by a river. Back there she was married, and her daughter, Philomena, was just starting to toddle. That's why she's glad she didn't go in the Lethe, so she can recognize her family when they come. She asks if there are more tools at the palace and I say I'll check, and then she turns to me and says, "Listen to me, rambling on. What's your name?"

Without thinking I answer, "Persephone," then catch my breath.

"Persephone? Just like the queen? That's funny."

What am I going to say? Do I tell her and have her go all scared and formal on me? I don't think so.

"Just like the queen."

"Two Persephones in one place! I guess you call her 'my lady.' And I bet she doesn't even know your name. Still, it's funny, isn't it?"

"Yes," I say. "It's hilarious."

139

So now I have a friend. And she's a mortal.

Is it so wrong, letting Melita think I'm mortal, too? She doesn't know who I am, and I don't want to tell her.

I came barefoot, holding my sturdy new spade. I saw her glance at my dress, its weave immeasurably finer than hers, and at the engraved brooches on my shoulders. But she thinks it's because I'm a servant in the palace, and I don't want to tell her otherwise.

She even said she saw the queen once, when she was finally called for greetings, but the throne room was so big and she felt so scared, all she noticed was a crown and a purple chiton.

Even then, I didn't tell her who I am. Because I've heard all the stories, how mortals act when they meet up with gods. They cower and swoon, or they try to win your favor. The last thing I need is someone fawning all over me like an overeager puppy begging for approval. I need a friend.

Still, sometimes I think of Zeus disguising himself as a swan, and I start to get a queasy feeling, the one that comes with questions I don't like. If I let Melita think I'm a servant, doesn't that make me one more opportunistic god in disguise?

And I always answer myself the same way. What I'm doing is completely different. I would never try to manipulate Melita. I just want someone to laugh with and work next to in the garden. Zeus left Leda laying an egg, but nothing I do could change Melita's fate: she's already dead.

No, everything will be fine. I can keep my immortality to myself. I'm not exactly brimming over with special powers, anyway.

The Present

I'm combing my hair when Hades walks into the bedroom. He comes up behind me and puts his warm hands on my shoulders, then leans down and kisses the nape of my neck.

"Someone's here to see you," he murmurs.

I put down my comb and stand up, turning to face him. I put my hands on his waist.

"Hello, someone," I say.

He chuckles. "No, not me! Hermes is back, and he brought you something. A gift. He won't show me what it is until you come down."

"Let him wait a little longer," I say, snuggling close.

But Hades whispers, "Later," and leads me to the door.

⁓※⁓

Hermes is sitting on one of the golden couches, unbuckling the wings from his sandals, when we come in. He looks up and smiles.

"Found you something interesting," he says.

He puts the wings in his sack, rummages around, and hands me a small woven bag. Hades and I sit on the couch opposite him and I open it. Inside is a wooden box tied with string.

"Didn't want them to squish," says Hermes, grabbing a cup of nectar from the tray and chugging it down. Hades offers me a drink as well, but I shake my head, intent on the box in my palm.

The string has a knot. Hermes pulls out his knife and hands it to me. When I pause for a moment, trying to figure out how to proceed, he laughs.

"You look like Pandora," he says.

"Who?"

"It was that eager expression of yours," he says. "Pandora was a mortal whose curiosity got the better of her. She opened a forbidden box and out flowed disease, poverty—all the woes afflicting mankind."

"What exactly have you put in there, Hermes?" jokes Hades.

"Stop it, you two," I say. "Let me open my present."

I flick the knife through the string and lift the lid.

"Hermes! Seeds for my garden! You're wonderful! What are they?"

"Damned if I know. Found them on one of my journeys. Those tiny black ones look like poppy seeds."

I poke around with my finger. "And this is definitely a plum pit. Oh, I'd love to grow a plum tree. Wait, there's one more stuck in the corner."

I wiggle something loose, then pick it up carefully and lay it in my palm: a pointy-edged oval, glistening and fat with shining red juice almost like blood.

"That one looks good enough to eat," says Hades, reaching over, but I close my fingers and pull my hand back.

"Oh, no you don't! That's getting planted. Let's see what it grows."

I make my grateful good-byes to Hermes, stop to grab a spade, and rush out to my garden.

Tactical Maneuvers

 $\mathcal{H}$ ades gave me a beautiful, ebony gaming table inlaid with ivory. My warriors are flat, round rubies. Hades' are onyx, carved with open gates. He rolls higher, so he gets the first move. As usual.

He places a piece on the board. Soon my men are trooping toward the center of the table, and Hades is building a phalanx at one end.

"Cowering at the back of the field!" I joke. "That's not like you."

"Nothing wrong with a good defensive position," he says.

I roll again. All my men are in and the board is wall-to-wall pieces. "It looks like the throne room," I say.

"You're doing very well there, by the way."

At first I think he means the game, but obviously not: I've left a gap and he moves in, isolating one of my men.

"I thought your words on the Lethe were nice and clear," he continues. "Much more informative than I tend to be. It's an improvement."

The praise tastes delicious. And maybe it's an opening for something that's been on my mind since I met Melita.

"You know," I say, "some shades are here for days before they come to the throne room."

I pause, examining the board. I realize I don't want to mention Melita's name or our friendship. Hades doesn't have friends among the shades. He might disapprove.

I move my piece. "That's a long time. I bet they feel lost and confused. I bet some of them end up in the Lethe by accident."

"We do greetings when we've got a roomful. It's a simple matter of managing our resources."

"Managing resources!" I put both my hands on the table and lean toward him. "Shades aren't resources! They're individuals, with thoughts and feelings. Haven't you ever wondered what it's like for them when they first get here?"

I look at his confident face. No, he hasn't thought about it.

He moves a man. "What are you proposing?"

"We need to do throne room greetings every day."

"Every day!"

"It doesn't take that long. And after the greetings, we could have guided tours, so shades learn where everything is, in case they're too nervous to hear what we say. And I'm thinking about a new arrivals list. Some of your 'resources' spend a long time waiting for those they love."

"Is that *all* you want?" He's raising that eyebrow, smiling.

I look at the board. How should I proceed? "It might make your work easier," I say, moving a burst of red into his crowd of onyx men. "The more comfortable shades are, the less trouble they'll cause."

He puts his elbow on the table and rests his chin on his hand. Is he thinking about my ideas or examining his position? Finally he says, "You have a point. With the scale of this drought they're more agitated than usual."

The drought.

"Your turn," says Hades.

But I don't move. I'm trying to see something bigger than the board. This isn't just about the crowds in the throne room or whether we have tours.

"What *is* happening on Earth?" I say. "We never talk about it."

"Are you going to roll?" he asks briskly.

I move a man for the sake of moving. "When you saw Hermes last night, did you discuss the drought? Or what's happening with the crops? Did he mention my mother?"

Hades hurls down the dice. Doubles. He forces a dark piece behind my open man.

"It doesn't matter," he says, "because we're not going to talk about Earth." With his next roll he cuts off my escape. "And I'll tell you why."

He lets go of the man and reaches to take my hand. He lowers his voice, softening it so it wraps around me. "I don't even want your thoughts up there. When it comes to you, I'm a very greedy man. This is your home now. You belong here by my side."

The game is over.

"Now," he says. "About those daily greetings . . ."

Melita's Story

Melita is straightforward and practical with plants, like a brisk mother duck keeping her ducklings in line. There's no nonsense in the way she trims a branch or plops a new plant in its freshly dug hole. It's so different from the way my mother caresses every leaf as if they were getting drunk together.

Now Melita is standing, hands on hips, in front of the bush that burst from the juicy, red seed.

"What do you want to plant near this?" she asks.

A hummingbird zips in front of her, hovers near a scarlet trumpet-blast of a flower, then darts its beak into the flaming center, searching for the sweetness hiding inside.

You've never seen anything grow as fast as this bush. It's already chest-high, with spiky little leaves jutting off everywhere. Green suckers crowd greedily from the base, as if it's too eager to settle for one trunk. Everything about it is uneven and sprouty, but I can't bring myself to trim it back. I love its exuberance—flowers already! It needs to keep sprouting and stretching until it figures out where it's going and why.

"Let's put a carpet of something low around it," I suggest. "Maybe mint. At this rate the bush will be taller than us in a month. Then we can move in some hyacinths or lavender."

"Lavender, so we can rub it on our hands and dresses! I used to do that for my daughter." She stops, looking inward with a sigh, then shakes her head. "At least my mother's there to do it for her now. She's taking good care of Philomena. I thank the gods for that."

She starts pulling up weeds from around the bush.

"Too bad we don't have goats," she says.

"What for?"

"To eat the weeds, of course. We had a herd back home. We named them after the gods. I hope you don't think that's rude. Zeus is the randy one. Athena's so smart, she always finds the path to the first flowers, the tenderest leaves. And we named Aphrodite because of her long, silky hair and her huge eyes. She has a son. He scrambles on the rocks like a bouncing spring, all four feet leaping at the same time. Once he even climbed on top of the big crag that rises behind our house. It's shaped like a rooster's comb. There he stood on the tallest of the five points, looking proud as could be. He's named Eros, of course."

"Eros the love goat!" I laugh. "That seems just right somehow."

She shrugs. "You know, their names aren't a joke. When their milk gushes into my bowl, all sweet and warm, it really is a gift from the gods. We make it into cheese, two kinds— one softer and one harder. The hard one ages longer, so it sells for more."

She looks up apologetically. "I guess my head's stuck back home today. Sorry."

"Melita, I love hearing about your life on Earth."

And that's the absolute truth. I'm greedy to know what it's like for mortals up there—the people my mother said need us like little children. Well, Melita certainly wasn't some helpless child. I want to learn everything I can.

"Tell me more about the cheese."

"The *cheese*?"

"Sure."

"My husband built a storeroom where we aged the rounds, lined up on shelves. All those perfect circles. Pick one up and sniff, and you can still make out the smell of sweet grass by the riverbank and the herbs that cling higher on the crags. That's where the goats go foraging. Athena always finds the sweet herbs first."

"Didn't you ever wish for an easier life?"

She shakes her head emphatically. "I wouldn't have traded it for anything in the world. My mother always said she's sorry I couldn't have been a fine lady in town. She hoped I'd marry someone richer. Attract a rich man, me? I'm no beauty. And I'm glad I didn't live that way, trapped in a house, never getting outside except for a festival day now and then. The only fresh air a rich woman gets is in her own courtyard. No, I liked working hard and being outside near the goats and the garden, like my mother always did. She taught me everything I needed to know."

Her voice slows down. "Sometimes I miss her so much, I think it's going to hollow me out inside."

I worry she's going to get moody and stop talking, so I prompt her. "Tell me about your husband."

"He's a good man. He cared for me. He let me keep Philomena, even though she was small and he hoped for a son. 'She can help with the goats soon enough,' he said. 'You don't have to be big for that.'"

"Let you *keep* her?"

"You always have to wonder, don't you? I mean, since fathers get to decide their babies' fates. My friend's husband made her leave her newborn on the hillside. He said they had too many mouths to feed already. And what good was another girl, who'd only go to her husband's family instead of staying to care for the farm? But my husband isn't like that. He's kind and hardworking. He built the cheese room as soon as he saw we needed the space. And he agreed right away when I begged him to let my mother move in with us. He said, 'We can use another pair of hands around here.'"

She checks that she hasn't missed a single weed, then starts separating some creeping mint to move over.

"And that was the truth, because the three of us worked from the second the old rooster crowed until we banked the embers in the hearth at night. When I had Philomena, my mother did her work and mine both. She never complained. She never once said, 'Hurry up and get to work.' No, she said, 'You stay there with your nursling, dear. You get her good and fat.' And then she'd go off washing, or cooking, or gathering firewood."

I've stopped working. I'm just sitting there listening. I can practically see Melita's mother bustling around, tending the fire, pausing only to gaze with warm eyes at her daughter and the newborn child.

"Does Philomena look like you?"

"She's much prettier. Her head is covered with dark ringlets, and her eyes are a rich green, like olives hanging on a tree in the sun. She was born with a mark on her shoulder that looks like a flower with four petals, so we call her our little blossom. You never saw such pink cheeks! It's a good life." Then she catches herself and adds, so softly I can barely hear her, "I mean, it was."

She pauses, nestling clumps of roots into their new spot. As she pats them down, she sighs, as if trying to settle herself back down, too.

"It couldn't stay like that forever," she goes on. "Everything changes, right? My husband heard they were looking for oarsmen, and he signed up. 'A year will go fast,' he said. 'You and your mother can care for the goats and the garden and the baby between you, and I'll come home with gold jingling in my pocket and we'll have a bigger farm.'

"What could I say to that? So off he went, taking those strong arms to work the oars day in and day out. I said to my mother, 'Won't he have nice shoulders when he comes back?' And she said, 'You're the lucky girl.'

"And it did go well, at first. Philomena grew plump, and in no time at all she was toddling after the goats. We piled cabbages in the storeroom and enough garlic and onions to see us through a winter. And my mother and I took our cheeses into market every market day. We came home with coins to put in a little red pot in the kitchen, to add to the bag of gold my husband would bring. And then . . ."

"Don't stop, Melita. And then what?"

"One day I was in the garden with Philomena, and I felt so dizzy I had to sit down. It came over me like a wave knocking me off my feet. My mother put her rough hand on my forehead. 'You're burning up, girl,' she said. 'In you go.'

"She took Philomena on her hip and put her other arm around my waist to prop me up, and we tottered like that into the house and over to my bed, my mother shooing the chickens out of the way.

"I could hardly sit up, it came on so fast. I was burning and coughing and the room was spinning. Sometimes I woke and the room was dark. Sometimes the sun was shining so hard it hurt my eyes, and my mother covered them with a damp strip of cloth. My bed was soaked through with sweat. When I woke my mother cooed, 'Never you worry, dear. Everything's fine. You just rest.'

"'But my baby!'

"'She's old enough for goat's milk. She won't go hungry. You sleep.'

"'But the garden! Milking!'

"'Everything's fine. You rest.'"

Melita lifts a corner of her chiton to wipe her eyes.

"And then one day I didn't wake up. No, that's not right. One day I felt clearheaded again. A man with wings was there saying, 'Let's go.'

"I pleaded with him not to take me. I told him my baby needed me to keep her safe, that she couldn't live without me.

"But he just said, 'Look,' and pointed. There was my mother, snoring away on her cot, with Philomena cuddled up in her arms as round and rosy as an apple. What could I say? Philomena will be all right. She has my mother to love her and feed her and teach her right from wrong, like she did for me. They'll hold on until my husband comes home."

I'm so deep in her story, I can't see anything but a simple bed; a strong, warm arm; and that dark-haired, pink-cheeked child.

Melita wipes a last tear away, and shakes her head firmly, as if to dislodge the sorrow. Then she says in a brisk, determined voice, "Haven't I gone on!" And the garden floods back to life around me.

"I know this sounds strange," I say, thinking out loud, "but do you ever think it might be good that you're here? You don't have to work so hard anymore. And you know your baby's well cared for, so you don't have to worry."

She stares at me. "Have you lost your mind? I'd be back with Philomena in a second. I miss hugging her all soft and warm, smelling the sweet milkiness of her. And I miss my mother so much! I ache for the way it felt when she put her arm around me and I knew she'd make everything all right. I'd be building my farm again with my own two hands if I could, and welcoming my handsome husband home."

So much to love—and to lose.

Too moved to say anything, I reach up and pluck one of the orange-red flowers from the bush. It's shapely, like a woman draped in a bright, snug dress. I trace the curve of her breasts and the wider curve of her hips, where the tight petals split, revealing a ruffled swirl of underskirts, dancing. One of the pesky hummingbirds comes exploring, so I swoosh him away, his quiet buzz the only sound.

I try to concentrate on my weaving, but the shuttle is playing tricks on me. Nothing's smooth today. I'm like a dog that keeps losing a scent and ends up circling back, lost and confused.

I can't stop thinking about Melita and her mother. And every time I see them together in my mind, I get the strangest feeling: prickly and sinking at the same time.

I didn't know anyone could welcome a mother's help that way.

I stop for the tenth time to untangle my thread, and suddenly I picture my mother's face. Just look at her! She's the epitome of a powerful woman. I think back to when I was little and I still used to beg her not to go off to the fields. Time and time again she explained how crucial her work was to the world, so she couldn't stay and talk. *Maybe after this festival, dear, or once harvest season is over.*

Sometimes mortals are the lucky ones.

Good Dogs

Rounded river pebbles mumble under my feet, and my collecting bag hangs eagerly at my side. The garden needs more reeds. Farther up the shore I see Charon's boat pulled up, and a second later I hear his rough voice.

"Good boys! Fetch it! Fetch!"

A gigantic dog leaps, its jaws grabbing a stick in midair. Then another mouth reaches over, tugging the stick to the side. A third head barks gleefully as the beast runs back up the beach and deposits the stick at Charon's feet.

"Good dogs," says Charon, bending to pick up the branch.

One of the dog heads whips up, sniffing. The other two heads follow. Then the dog is bounding my way. There's no mistaking those three heads, those powerful jaws. I've seen them embellished in gold on Hades' chariot and carved on the arms of my throne.

"Stop!" shouts Charon in a frantic voice, waving the stick over his head as if to keep the dog from attacking. He pants in pursuit, but the dog's long legs move like the wind, and the ferryman is rapidly losing ground.

He's still struggling up the shore when the dog skids to a stop in front of me, eager and playful. I hold out my hand for each of the three heads to sniff. The right head licks my hand, and I scratch it behind the ears. Then the beast is jostling me like a gigantic puppy. He flops on his back with all four huge feet in the air, and I scratch his tummy. He kicks his hind feet in pleasure.

Charon arrives, gasping for breath. "Careful there! Step back!"

The dog rolls over and sits by my side.

"I never." Charon's bushy eyebrows meet in consternation. "He don't do that with nobody but me, and him and me, we've known each other forever."

The dog reaches over, grabs Charon's stick, and begins to worry the wood with his teeth.

"Is *this* Cerberus?" I ask.

He nods. "Cerberus, Guardian of the Dead."

"Some guardian!" I laugh as the right head rubs against my side, begging for another scratch.

Charon's brow is a confusion of wrinkles. "I never seen him like this with nobody before. You don't want to be there when he's doin' his job. Those three mouths drippin' blood and strips of flesh, those six eyes drunk with death—it's like the furies themselves settle into his soul."

"I didn't know people were so eager to get in here," I joke. "It seems kind of silly to kill them to keep them out."

"Keep 'em out! Girl, his job is to keep 'em in. Look at you, forgettin' already what I told you back in the boat that one time. No one goes back. Once you're here, you're here. Them that think they still got business on the other side, Cerberus tells 'em different pretty quick. Three days ago the picture wasn't so pretty. She was a young one. Not much older than you. They say she left a sweetheart on the other side. Never stopped cryin'. Didn't give the Lethe a chance to wash her clean. She just plunged into the Styx and started flailin' across. I don't know how, but she made it to the other shore."

Charon pauses. His mouth narrows into a grim line. "Cerberus was standin' there, pullin' his lips back and barin' his fangs, those three heads rumblin' all together like a volcano. But it was like she was in a dream and couldn't see him. She kept goin'. He leaped; knocked her flat. And then those heads was rippin' and snarlin'. Bits of flesh sprayed around like raindrops."

He shakes his head. "Once he does that, the screams

don't last long. Ravens land in the trees, waitin' for their turn. Cerberus ain't done till there's nothin' bigger than this here stick, bones and all. Then the fire dies out of his eyes. He swims back over here. The river washes off the blood, the little bits of skin. He climbs out and gives a shake, lookin' all pleased with himself."

Cerberus knows we're talking about him, and he holds his heads high. He pushes against my hand again until I scratch under one of his collars.

"Well, I never," says Charon. "I never."

He looks over at those teeth, longer than my fingers, still playing with the remnants of the splintered stick.

"If he's so dangerous," I ask, "why didn't he attack me? Is it because I wasn't in the water?"

"You was lucky today, girl. I don't know why. But be careful, you hear me?"

Famine and Feast

I'm finally getting used to the throne room. I have to admit it's taken a while. After my "grand entrance," I didn't want to go back at all. Just thinking about it made me feel like crabs were scuttling across my skin. But each time is easier than the one before, and now the path to the throne doesn't even make my heart beat faster.

Today I'm wearing my orange and saffron chiton and the golden earrings curved like Charon's boat, a small figure with a sailor's cap perched in the prow. And the new sandals I requested. Their tops are adorned with plenty of diamonds so when I put my feet on the royal footstool, they flash in proper regal splendor, but their soles are plain old leather.

Hermes, wings still on his ankles, leans against a pillar as the mortal shades bow low. It's a huge crowd today.

We bid them rise and then say words of welcome. We point out the guides who will show them around. I describe the Rivers of Forgetting and Fire, and Hades warns them that Cerberus guards the Styx. He closes with the now familiar words, "There is no going back. Cerberus will not let you pass. This is your home now."

Usually, the shades listen reverently, awed by our presence and overwhelmed by the newness of it all. But today the stillness is broken by a stage whisper.

"Who'd want to go back to that mess?"

Every head turns. There, in the middle of the great hall, stands a sturdy, scruffy farmer with a well-lined face. Next to him, a scrawny woman grabs his arm as if to pull him back from notice.

But if he's willing to talk, I'm eager to listen. Each day, as the crowds before me grow larger, Earth and the drought weigh heavier on my mind. I want to know what brought these shades here and what they had to leave behind.

I glance at Hades; he's in an excellent mood today. He won't mind my asking just this once. In what I hope is a reassuring voice, I ask the farmer to step forward and describe what's happening on Earth.

He hesitates, but the woman beside him hisses, "Now you got yourself into it, you might as well speak up!"

The farmer takes a few steps and spreads his feet wide, as if planting himself to resist a powerful wind. "It hasn't rained in months," he says. "It stopped raining right when the new shoots were rising. They withered to nothing. I touched them and they crumbled like flakes of ash. We used what water we had—"

"But that water ran away faster than a boy skipping out on chores," his wife butts in, obviously accustomed to making their sentences a joint endeavor. "Even the deep-down water dried up. The cows ate the grass down to dirt and then kicked the dirt away. Clouds of dust everywhere, and so many cracks in the ground, you couldn't walk without tripping."

"How long did you say it was since the last rain?" I ask.

"Months," says the farmer.

"And when did you last sacrifice to Demeter?"

Hades shifts uncomfortably on the throne beside me.

"Last week," says the farmer, "but it wasn't much of a sacrifice. There's not enough left to offer up."

"We may be poor, but we're not stupid!" the woman exclaims. "Of course we sacrificed to Demeter, but it's like she's gone deaf or something. We prayed, we begged, we pleaded. Nothing."

"Even sacrificed the last of the cows a while ago," says the farmer. "We usually offer the goddess grain and wine, but we thought something special would get her attention, maybe tell her how much we were hurting. Nothing changed, except no more trickles of milk."

His wife sighs and shakes her head. "It's simple. No rain means no food. It means hearing hungry children cry. No, we're happy enough to be here. Someone said there's going to be a banquet."

She whispers in the farmer's ear. He bows clumsily. I nod to the guides, and they start gathering people into groups.

I turn to Hades and ask softly, "How much worse can it get up there?"

He shrugs, not answering.

I know, I know. He doesn't want to talk about Earth. But the farmer put a face on the suffering, and I need some help making sense of this. "What is my mother thinking?" I persist. "These people don't look like they've even been disrespectful, let alone sinful."

"It's not so bad that we're busy, you know," Hades says. "Things are booming around here! But let's talk about it later. They're heading off to the banquet."

Perhaps he's right. This is a very public place. I'll wait—as long as we really do talk later.

I pull my thoughts back to the room before me. "I've always thought this part of the welcoming is nice," I whisper, "having a banquet when shades arrive."

"Nice doesn't have much to do with it. The food binds them to the underworld."

He reaches over and starts running his fingers up and down my bare arm. His voice turns playful. "Perhaps you'd like to join them? I know you don't need to eat, except for pleasure." The fingers draw flirtatious circles. "You are immortal, after all. Still, I haven't noticed you nibbling anything down here. A nice hunk of bread, perhaps, and some sweet fig jam, to keep you by my side forever?"

I shake my head at him and smile. "Not right now. Besides, you don't need any tricks to keep me here. I love you. I've chosen my life."

Now his fingers wander over to my thigh.

"No tricks at all?" he murmurs in that low, intimate voice.

I feel myself warming from head to toe.

"Still blushing, my bride?"

And I wish we weren't in the throne room and that night's welcoming curtains were drawing closed around us.

But no such luck. Hermes detaches himself from his pillar and comes striding over, totally oblivious to the heat hovering around the throne.

"Another day, another crowd," he says. "I'm so busy, it's taking all the fun out of my work. I could use a drink. Where are you hiding the nectar?"

Hades signals to a servant. I shake myself; the spell is broken.

"Hermes, you drink so much, we're going to need

another storeroom just for you!" I laugh. Then something occurs to me. "Come to think of it, you ate all those grapes in my garden, too. And yet you cross the Styx all the time. Doesn't food bind *you* to the underworld?"

"I'm the exception," he says with a grin. "Travel is in my job description. I go everywhere."

It seems like rules are riddled with exceptions.

"Then you must see everything," I go on. There aren't any shades around now. Hades won't mind one more quick question about Earth, will he? "Tell me, how bad are things getting up there?"

"Bad. I've never seen it like this. It's so dry, even the gods have started griping to Zeus. Like the mortal said, there aren't enough animals left to sacrifice. Ah, what I'd give for some nice fatty smoke wafting up from the sacrificial flames!"

He pulls off his hat and runs his fingers through his golden curls. "And Zeus—I've never seen him so out of sorts. He's ordering me around more than ever, trying to prove he's still boss of something. 'Hermes, go here! Hermes, one more thing!' No, I try to stay out of his way as much as I can. He's as brittle as the twigs that used to be fruit trees."

"This can't keep up," I say, trying to convince myself. "It's bound to rain soon, don't you think?"

No one answers.

Hades puts a hand on our guest's shoulder, steering him

to the door, and raises an eyebrow to ask if I'll join them. I shake my head.

Once they're gone, I sit on the steps leading down from the throne. The room is empty.

"Let's talk about it later," he said.

Every time I mention Earth, Hades changes the subject. What were his words? "I don't even want your thoughts up there." As if thinking about Earth will make me so mopey, I can't do my job properly here. But he's wrong. It's *not* knowing that's distracting me. I should tell him that.

I need to set my thoughts straight. That way, next time we're alone, I won't get confused and lose track of the conversation.

I try to separate the voices mumbling in the back of my head. *Birds devouring seed grain . . . crops withering to dust . . . mortals sacrificing to my mother, her ears as deaf as stone . . .*

How can people atone for their sins if she won't listen?

The odd thing is, she seemed so happy with mortals after the Thesmophoria. She was beaming about their grateful worship, their bounteous offerings, that smirking pig. And then I came here and everything started to change.

Then I came here. . . .

Maybe this isn't about mortals at all.

The room starts to grow chilly. I hug my arms across my chest.

The drought started when I came.

It's a coincidence! My mother wouldn't harm her precious crops on my behalf. Her priorities have always been clear. She used to smile when she stood in fields of waving grain. When she stood next to me, she was usually frowning.

I didn't tell her I was leaving.

Look, she's obviously angry about something, but it can't be because of me. And there's not much I can do from down here, anyway. Earth is Zeus's realm. He'll step in if things get bad enough.

How bad is bad enough?

I stand back up. I'm not doing such a good job sorting things out. And the more I think about it, the less I'm sure I want to. Or that I need to. Hades doesn't seem concerned, after all. And it's bound to rain soon.

I head up to my room to change, hoping the voices won't follow me there.

Not-So-Long-Lost Love

Melita sees my face. "What's the matter?"

"It's my mother. I'm afraid she's—" I stop cold.

"Still back on Earth, is she?"

I clamp my mouth and nod. I don't want to say more, because I'm afraid I'll talk myself into a corner.

The look she gives me is full of compassion. "I know," she says softly. "Everything is rotten up there right now. But if you haven't seen her here, chances are she's fine."

She grabs my hand. "I can't believe how selfish I've been! I just kept blabbing about my family and never once asked who you left behind. Tell me about your mother now. It will make you feel better."

I shake my head frantically.

"I bet she has someone to keep an eye on her, right?" she goes on. "Like Philomena—she has my mother. I know because I've been looking around and I haven't seen my mother here yet. And my husband will be back at the farm soon enough, and he can take care of everyone, family and goats alike."

She spurts out a laugh. "That makes me remember a song he used to sing. This will take your mind off anything!"

She starts teaching me a ballad about a wayward goatherd and his gullible sweetheart. I start to sing along, and soon, with every rowdy verse, I'm guffawing in a distinctly un-ladylike manner. It's lucky I made this garden down the path from the palace and not right up where everyone can see me. Melita was right: the song is doing a great job of making me forget my worries.

We're calming down and getting back to work when an ancient man toddles over to the bench and sinks down slowly. I hold a finger to my lips and Melita nods. We'll give him some silence.

The garden starts to work its magic on him.

"Ah, the peace! The quiet!" He sighs. "No more, 'Why aren't you working faster? Can't you do any better?' Finally."

He closes his eyes and lifts his face, soaking up solitude and sun.

Turning to grab my trowel, I see newcomers coming out from the palace with their guides. I feel a flush of pride. It's one of the tours I started to help shades learn their way around.

One group heads down toward the Lethe's grassy banks. As they pass within glancing distance of the garden, a very round woman stops and stares in our direction. She clamps little triangles of arms on her hips, then her hands fly up, and a faint shout drifts through the air. She looks like a stumpy, overfed toad, and Melita and I start giggling again. But the old man doesn't hear anything. He's intent on the music the bees make drowsing through the bushes.

The roly-poly woman starts rushing toward us, pulling her skirts up so she can run faster. She gains momentum like a rock tumbling downhill. Soon we can see her creased red face and her screeches grow louder and louder.

"There you are! Don't you try to hide from me. You come help me this minute!"

The old man moans, his eyes still closed, as if in a bad dream.

"Thought they could palm me off on that guide, did they?" shrieks the toad. "But a guide can't help me with these achy old legs. Come help me! Now!"

The man opens his eyes. The woman is no dream. He lurches up, grabs his cane, and starts to hobble—but in the opposite direction! She's gaining. He tosses the walking stick aside and starts a lopsided run.

Melita and I clamp our hands over our mouths, trying not to laugh out loud. But that tornado of a woman wouldn't hear us no matter what we do.

"You come back here, you old good-for-nothing! Come help me drag these ailing bones."

The old man flees toward the Lethe as fast as his rickety legs will carry him. Like an army scouring the countryside, she surges in his wake, flattening grasses and bushes as she goes. The gap narrows.

"Don't you recognize me?" she hollers. "It's me, your sweetie pie!"

Melita's shoulders are shaking like leaves in a windstorm, and my eyes are watering. Our laughter finally explodes, blasting our hands away. After a while I begin to catch my breath. Then I see Melita hugging her sides, gasping, "It's me, your sweetie pie!" And I'm off again.

It feels so good. I wish I could laugh like this forever.

"Well, it *would* have been a nice place for him to rest," says Melita, collapsing on her back in the grass.

Arachne

"We've done wonders here, Melita."

I'm sitting near the bush with spiky leaves. The red flowers have all fallen, giving way to a single, bulging fruit. A few days ago Melita finally recognized it. It's called a pomegranate.

At first, the fruit was yellowish green, speckled with just a few red dots. Its tiny body, hard as a pebble, was overpowered by the spiky crown of a calyx it wore on the dangling end. But the calyx stayed the same size while the fruit grew and grew, and now the pomegranate is as big as an apple and turning redder by the day. Soon it will be nothing but a great stretched belly with a teeny tiara perching on top.

I run my fingers along its rough, uneven hide. "Come on, Melita, admit it. This garden is amazing. Mo—I mean, Demeter herself couldn't do better."

"Hush!"

I plop over on my elbows. "What are you so worried about? Everything is growing in the most amazing way. There's no denying it."

She nods. "It does seem like everything sprouts or blossoms the second we touch it. The soil must be really rich. Still . . ." With nervous fingers, she smoothes her chiton over her knees, rearranging the folds so it looks orderly again. "Still, it's dangerous to boast. The gods might hear us."

"So what?"

"Oh, Persephone, don't! Think about what happened to Arachne when she boasted."

"Who?"

"Arachne, the weaver who said she was as good as the goddess Athena. You know the story."

"As a matter of fact, I don't."

"Where on earth did you grow up? Everyone knows this story."

All right, so maybe I didn't always pay attention. I'm listening now.

"Hurry up and tell it to me."

She smooths her skirts again and sits up straight,

composing her face and her thoughts. When she starts to talk again, it's in the singsong voice of someone reciting from memory.

"Once there was a girl named Arachne, who was born knowing how to weave. From an early age she spun the smoothest thread and pulled the shuttle in true, straight lines. When other girls her age were just learning to wind yarn into balls, she was already weaving patterns so complicated, even the old women came to stare in wonder."

"Quite the prodigy," I say.
Melita shushes me, then continues.

"News of Arachne's talents spread, and by the time she was a young woman, even the nymphs snuck out of the forests to watch her work. As the crowds grew, so did Arachne's pride.

"One day a flower nymph, lured from her field by the pleasure of watching Arachne's quick fingers, said, 'Oh, great is Athena, who gave you this gift!'

"Arachne turned and glared. 'Athena? She had nothing to do with it. The gift is my own. Why, the goddess could take lessons from me.'

"With a gasp of alarm, the crowd stepped back.

Only one person stayed close to the loom: an old woman shrouded in black. 'Beware,' she croaked. 'Athena watches over the ways of the loom and the household; her talents put yours to shame. Give the gods their due respect.'

"Arachne put one hand on her hip and smirked. 'I don't think the gods are due a thing. If Athena really thinks her weaving is better than mine, she should come here and we'll have a contest. Then we'll see whose fingers are nimbler.'

"'Have your wish, foolish girl!' cried the old woman, dropping her black cloak.

"Now the crowd shook and fell to its knees, for the woman grew younger and more beautiful before their eyes, until finally she stood towering over their heads, shining with an inner light. Yes, it was Athena herself."

Oh, no. Not the towering, shining thing. "The show-off," I say.

Melita gives me a little shove. "Do you want to hear the rest or not?"

I fold my hands meekly in my lap and nod like a good student.

Melita takes a deep breath, then resumes her singsong voice.

❧✦❧

"Two looms sprang up before them. The woman stood at one, the goddess at the other. They wove and they wove and they wove some more, and the crowd gasped in wonder at the pictures flowing like magic from their hands.

"Athena's handiwork glowed with the gifts she gives to mankind. The owl, reminding us of her wisdom, stood in the center. Surrounding the intricate feathers of its wings, women cooked and wove and sewed. Each was so lifelike, you could almost see her breath.

"The goddess was tying off her last string when Arachne cried, 'There!'

"And on Arachne's loom . . ."

Melita stops and shivers, so I prod her on with a look.

"On Arachne's loom, gods debased themselves with lust and greed and jealousy. Zeus, the greatest god of all, was shown in ridiculous disguises stealing mortal women away. Hera, his wife, was goggle-eyed with accusations, and Poseidon romped about in compromising positions with various creatures of the sea."

❧✦❧

I start to laugh, then turn it into a cough. She keeps going, staring at me hard so I'll listen.

"But that wasn't the worst. No: Arachne had dared to create a finer weave and more vivid pictures than the goddess herself. Every detail, every expression on every face, every strand of her work was perfect.

"Rage darkened Athena's eyes. She raised her shuttle, suddenly as sharp as a sword, and slashed Arachne's work to shreds. Then the goddess turned to Arachne herself.

"Once, twice, three times the shuttle came down on Arachne's head. With the first blow, the girl's skin turned hard and shiny. With the second blow, she began to shrink smaller and smaller, until her body was no larger than a pea. With the third blow, her arms and legs sucked up into the bloated, round little body, until only eight fingers waved at her sides.

"'If your fingers are so nimble, then weave!' cried Athena.

"And Arachne began to create the finest silk ever seen. To this day, her fingers never stop weaving, for she's the lowly spider. Each time we sweep her webs away, we remember her terrible sin."

Melita's words hang in the air, and for a minute everything is still. She nods, glad to have imparted this wisdom. But when she finally looks at me, her eyes narrow, because I'm angrily ripping leaves into a pile of jagged shreds.

You see, I've met Athena a few times. She used to come spend an afternoon in the vale every now and then, and she was always friendly and clever. I even looked up to her. Now, my image of her lies as shredded as these leaves.

"How could a goddess be so petty?" I ask.

"Persephone! Arachne deserved everything she got."

"Just because a mortal does something as well as a god—"

"Stop it! They might hear."

"So power grants the right to be selfish, is that it? To win every contest and be best every time? Don't mortals count for anything at all?"

"The gods can do with us what they like. Why would you want to bring that anger down on your head or on those you love?"

She stops for a moment, staring at me, and when she starts again, her voice is as taut as a bowstring. "What if I angered the gods and they took it out on my daughter? What if she went hungry? What if she became somebody's slave, and I heard she was being beaten, or worse? I couldn't stand it. I think I'd lose my mind."

She shakes her head firmly. "That's why I always play by their rules. You'll do the same if you know what's good for you. You may be dead, but you're not out of their reach."

"But that doesn't make it right. Gods demand respect from you, but they don't respect you in return. It isn't fair. Go on, admit it: it isn't fair."

But Melita is like a rock, stubborn and unmovable. She won't admit a thing.

My weaving is all snaggy this afternoon. Nothing is going right. I can't stop thinking about Arachne, and every time I see her fingers flailing around that little pea body, my yarn tangles.

It's almost like the gods are weaving with sinew and heartbeats. A flick of the wrist, a pass of the shuttle, and a mortal life is changed forever.

I stop to tug out a knot.

Look at Zeus, king of the gods. A fine example he sets, deceiving pretty girls with his elaborate disguises. Seduction is just a game for him, and mortals, his playthings. I wonder what would happen if he actually made friends with a human, like I'm friends with Melita. I've heard her stories; I've imagined living her life. So, no sinew and heartbeats for me. The only thing I'm weaving is this bedspread.

Again, my shuttle rows back and forth across the loom, jumbling spring blossoms with summer's ripe plums, nestling river reeds among mountain pansies, defying borders of place and time.

Borders. Boundaries.

You know, I think I understand how mortals feel, and not just from listening to Melita. After all, I spent most of my life with my mother. Talk about someone who needs to control things! I can practically hear her voice now: "Isn't it time you cleaned your room? That color is too light for your dark hair. Stand up straight—you look like a mollusk that strayed from its shell!"

She had to snip and prune every little thing about me. Why couldn't she just let me be myself? Why couldn't she let me go?

My hand stops again. This time, the strings I'm trying to untangle are all in my head:

A spider, eight fingers waving frantically at her sides;
The farmer planting his feet in that crowded room;
Shutters banging in the wind of my mother's anger . . .

The thoughts I'd tried to push away in the throne room start spinning into one thick thread, and then the thread is weaving its own hideous tapestry, lightning fast, before my unwilling eyes. I see crops withered to dust, and children with jutting ribs, and graves, hundreds and thousands of graves, and all because—

A volcano of hot, ugly truth surges through my body.

Because of me.

I'm the reason people are dying.

The shuttle drops from my hand. I feel so dizzy, I stagger, grabbing the loom so I won't fall.

My mother is trying to force me back to Earth! That's why she's causing the drought, to make my choice simple. Either I find my way to the vale, or every single living thing shrivels and dies.

How could I have been so blind? The truth has been staring me in the face, and I just squeezed my eyes shut because it was easier to pretend my mother didn't care. But she cares, all right. She cares that I've defied her, that I'm living my own life, becoming someone in spite of her. She cares about getting what she wants, which is showing me my place.

My breath is so fast I can barely think. What makes her assume I can cross the Styx? Cerberus would tear me to bits, and the ravens would peck at my shredded flesh for the rest of eternity. And even if I could go back, I don't *want* to. I don't want to sleep in my skinny old bed, under my mother's watchful eye, that tight smile showing how much she relishes her return to power.

Because that's what this is about: power. When Athena smashed her shuttle down on Arachne, she was saying the same thing: *You think that body is yours to control? Think again.*

Something starts to build in me. It rises up from the ground, through my feet, my legs, tightens in my arms, gathers in my lungs, until a single word bursts out and reverberates through the room so loud, the loom quivers.

"No!"

This body *isn't* hers, it's mine! I have a home here, and my husband and—

My husband. As soon as I think the words, panic gives way to a flutter of hope. I don't have to solve this! Hades, Lord of the Underworld, ruler of one third of all creation—if anyone is clever enough and strong enough to face my mother, it's him.

I race out the door and down the corridor.

In the throne room, the workrooms, the storage rooms—nothing. I grab one servant after another. *Have you seen Hades?* Gone. I dash out the door, across the forecourt, over to the stables. The horses stand in their stalls nibbling oats. They feign ignorance. But one of the stalls is empty.

I sprint outside and scan the horizon. He could be anywhere. I need someone to harness a horse—how hard can it be to ride on my own? Finally, I spot a stable hand and run over, but when I grab his arm, he shrinks back in fear. "No one but Himself rides the horses," he cries, quaking. "Not even you."

Back to the palace. Still no Hades. I try to calm down. He'll be back this evening, I tell myself. It's not long now, only a few hours, and he'll know what to do. We can't let her kill any more people. Maybe Hades can cross to Earth, or at least send a message with Hermes, and when Zeus sees what's happening, he'll force my mother to make it rain. She'll have to accept my marriage, my new life.

I tell the servants to fetch me the moment Hades returns. I go to our room to wait, but I can't sit still. I pace between the windows and the wall like a caged wildcat, back and forth so many times it should wear a path in the marble.

A knock. I run to the door, fling it open—a servant. Hades has sent word not to wait up. He'll be very late. Do I want anything sent to my room? No, nothing.

Hours later I stop pacing. I climb under the covers. I think I won't fall asleep. I think wrong.

It's morning when I wake. The bed beside me is still empty. But there's such a clamor and shouting outside, I jump up and fling open the shutters. Below my window and across the forecourt, shades are embracing, calling to each other, waving friends over to share news. I dash to the door and call, and a servant comes running. I ask her what's going on outside.

"My lady, the latest arrivals have brought news. It's raining on Earth—buckets and buckets of rain!"

Rain

Melita runs over and wraps me in a gigantic hug, twirling me around in her strong arms until my feet fly off the ground.

"Did you hear?" Her eyes glow like the sun. "Did you hear? It's raining on Earth!"

"Waterfalling! Practically cascading!"

"You and your fancy words. Plain old rain is good enough for me."

It seems the drought has lifted with a vengeance. Earth's skies are black with thunderclouds. Rain is pounding down so ferociously, the soil is like a sated sponge struggling to soak it all up. It's almost as if Zeus heard my thoughts yesterday, because it's obvious he talked to my mother and made her see reason.

Last night I was frantic beyond words, but now I'm actually relieved Hades was out so late. I don't need to bother him after all. There's no need to make a scene. Everything's going to be fine.

Melita raises her hands to the sky, beaming in gratitude. "Do you know what this means?" she says. "Green grass for the goats to eat, and plenty of vegetables to stock the larder, and people with enough money to buy cheese. And when my husband comes home, he'll find Philomena fat and happy!"

I feel as light as Melita looks. There will be enough water for every child and animal and stalk of grass. Seeds will burst open, sending out greedy roots. Calves will nuzzle their mothers' sides. Tables will groan under platters of meat and olives and eggs and figs and bread. Now no one will have to suffer in my name.

"Let's celebrate," I say. "This garden will welcome back her sisters on Earth. Are there berries yet? We'll have our own feast."

"It's high time you ate something from the garden!" says Melita. "But the grapes are all gone, and the plums are still hard and green. No, this is the only thing that looks ripe enough."

She stops in front of the pomegranate bush. The solitary fruit dangles like a big red ball, arcing its branch low. The spiky calyx stretches toward the earth, a chariot hanging from a glowing harvest moon.

But when I walk closer, the round ball becomes lumpy. Solid red paint separates into crimson dots stippled on a yellow base.

How could I have thought, even for a second, that it was all even and perfect and simple? Nothing ever is. Like my life, for instance. I remember when Melita said she saw the queen—saw me—and all she noticed was a purple gown. That's what mortals can make out, from far away, a perfect being clad in priceless garments. But approach the throne and you can hear my breath. Yes, I'm actually breathing. Come close enough to look in my heart: what a rough, uneven place that is these days.

I reach up to test the pomegranate's heft, but the spiky calyx jabs into my palm. I spread my fingers wide so the little crown slips through, and then I lift carefully. That's as close to cradling as it will let me get.

My fingers tighten around its curves. I want to pluck the fruit and see what's under that tough hide, but something tells me it has to guard its secrets until they're sweet enough to emerge.

"I bet it's supposed to be heavier," I say, letting go. "Maybe it will fall off by itself when it's ready."

"Then let's pick some flowers and weave them into crowns for our hair," says Melita.

Bright orange crocuses, delicate white daisies—we slip stem into slotted stem as the fountain sings of the glories, the wonders, of rain.

And More Rain

I stretch out in the curved red tub, luxuriating as warm water caresses my skin. Every drop feels delicious today, and I stay in longer than usual, dunking my head under again and again. When I come out, I'm anointed with oils smelling of just-opened flowers, and my skin glows, reflecting the light. When it's time to choose a chiton, I point to one I've never worn before: a bright blue with waves cresting along the hem. No sun-hot rubies for me today; I want all my jewelry to be lapis, as shining as lakes, as bounteous as rivers. Necklaces, earrings, brooches—I sparkle blue all over.

Hades strides in to see if I'm ready. I shoo out the servant girls and hold out my wrists for him to fasten the bracelet clasps. Then I throw my clattering arms around his neck and smile up at him.

"Isn't it wonderful?" I say. "It's finally raining!"

He gives me a small, strained smile, followed by a perfunctory peck on the lips. Then he walks to the window and gazes down. I join him, following his eyes to my garden, spreading rich and luxuriant. Every week there's a larger swath of green holding sway against the brown scrub grass.

"Soon Earth will look like that again," I say.

He's silent. I glance over and his lips are set, almost petulant—an expression I've never seen on him before.

"Come," he says. "We're late for the throne room."

We walk toward the door and it swings open by itself; it's a trick he has.

As we head down the hall, I chatter on eagerly. "I can hardly wait for greetings today! I'm going to ask the shades what it's like, with the rain. Maybe Earth is already green. Everything's going to be better now! Too many people were coming here too early."

"And why, pray tell, is that a problem?" His voice is hard, joyless.

His words shock me to the bone and I stop, stunned. Hades keeps walking.

By the time I catch up, we're in front of the throne room doors. Before I can ask if I heard him right, the doors open and he takes my arm, leading me in.

❧❦

For such a celebratory day, the crowd is oddly silent. Shades stand shoulder to shoulder, pinched for space in spite of the chamber's size. When we take our seats, there's barely room for them to bow.

Hades gives the welcoming speech by himself. I have to wave him on when he turns to me, because I'm too confused. What did he mean back in the hall? Doesn't he want the suffering to stop?

He's about to dismiss everyone to the banquet when I finally find my voice.

"Tell us about Earth," I say, raising my head to look out over the throng. "Is the rain helping yet? Is the soil ready for planting?"

"Soil?" asks a brawny man. "What soil? The rain is blasting down so hard, the fields are under water."

A gray-haired woman shuffles forward. "It's not just the fields," she says. "Everything is flooding. A mud slide washed my town away. We're all here now. Every last one of us."

Flooding? Mud slides? The words prick me, as sharp as brooches too hastily fastened. This is all wrong.

"I tried to make it to the mountains, but I ended up here instead," says a shade.

My hand is gripping the arm of the throne. It's almost as if the rain were a weapon instead of a blessing. . . .

"The mountains? That wouldn't have helped you. That's where I'm from," comes another voice. "Water is bursting down the ravines like stampeding bulls."

The voices and faces around me are dissolving into a blur. Desperation wells in my eyes, rises in my throat. This rain is no gift of reconciliation. No; it's just another tactic in my mother's plan. Drought wasn't working fast enough for her liking. She isn't going to stop until she's forced me back.

I was wrong to fall asleep last night! I should have stayed up and told Hades everything! I need to talk with him right now, this minute, and explain what's behind all this. He'll know what to do.

I turn to him, grabbing his hand, but when I see his expression, my words freeze.

He's smiling.

"You're *happy*?" I cry, throwing down his hand.

"Calm down," he says sharply. "Not here."

"Yes, here! Earth is washing away and you're *happy*?"

"Earth isn't my realm. It isn't my place to fix it." His smile has disappeared. "We'll talk later."

"We never talk later!"

But even as the words ring in the air, a horrible realization is shoving its way into my head. I jump to my feet.

"You *want* everyone to die!"

Hades surges up from the throne to tower over me. His voice booms across the room, shaking the rafters.

"OF COURSE I WANT PEOPLE TO DIE! I'M LORD OF THE DEAD! THAT'S WHO I RULE!"

A collective gasp rises from the crowd. Most of the shades fall to their knees.

But I'm not giving up. "And more death gives you more power. Is that it? Is that what you want?"

"Yes, by Cerberus!" he thunders back. "It gives me power. It gives *us* power. And there's nothing wrong with that."

Each word hits me like a blow.

The guides start scurrying around, shepherding shades toward the doors and away from our shouting match.

"But everyone is suffering! These are *people*, Hades, with names and lives and children. You need to help me. I need to go back to Earth and—"

"You're not going!" His voice is an iron gate slamming shut. "And we won't discuss this again."

He turns from me and strides down the steps, out the door.

"Oh, yes we will!" I shout after him. But my husband, the power-hungry tyrant, is already gone.

Only a Mother

I rip off the clanking jewelry and dump it on my floor, then bury it under the cursed blue chiton. Waves. Water. Like that was going to be the solution to everything.

I need to get out of this palace and into my garden where I can breathe again. All the way down the hall I'm swearing under my breath.

The years my mother spent trimming my branches weren't enough for her. No, she's got to yank me up by my roots and pound me back down where she thinks I belong. How could she do this? How? Does she have any idea how many people she's killed in her little game?

I shudder, and I don't know if it's from anger or fear.

There's my mother, flinging her power around like thunderbolts, and there's Hades, enjoying the results, and then there's me. Me, as blind as a mole, pretending I'm making things better for mankind with my stupid little garden and my stupid little questions from the throne. As if they made a difference to anyone.

I come stomping into the garden so hard, I practically crash into the pomegranate bush, and damn if that red orb doesn't plop right off its stem and land in a cushion of mint below.

"Well," says Melita, "look what just blew in."

She picks up the pomegranate, sheltering it in her hands, then looks back up at me. "What happened to you?"

"We were wrong. It's not better. Nothing's better." I crumple to the ground. The downpour, the flooded fields, whole towns slipping away—I describe it all.

"Are you sure? Were you there in the throne room? Did they let you come in?"

"I was there. I heard it with my own ears. What am I going to do?"

She puts down the pomegranate and reaches for my hand. "Do? We can't do anything but pray. Me, I'll pray my family is safe in the mountains. I'll pray my husband reaches home. I'll pray the gods can save them."

"Save them? What makes you think that's what they want to do?"

Suddenly I need to tell her everything. Melita, with her big fat heart and her common sense. She knows me so well; maybe, just maybe, she'll still love me in spite of my immortality. She's the only one in this whole mess who listens to me. She'll help me figure out what to do.

Or she'll leave.

Take your pick.

I try to open my mouth. Nothing comes. A nutshell too green to crack. A clam smothered in seaweed.

She shakes her head at my stuttering, then stands and pulls me up. She grabs a collecting bag and a spade. "You need something to do," she says. "Keep your hands busy and you won't have time to worry. Come on, we're going collecting."

She steers me downhill, toward the Lethe. "I saw a patch of white anemones the other day, near that pale poplar. There are plenty to spare for the garden. Come on."

With every step I'm struggling to find my words. As we near the Lethe's undulating banks, its voice gets louder, that soft, seductive song promising a perfect embrace, calling me to step closer, closer, closer—

"No!" I jerk to a stop. Words come out but not the ones I wanted. "I can't go any farther."

Or I might go in.

"Too tired?"

"I just can't."

"Then wait here for a minute. We're so close. I'll go dig up a few plants, and we'll head back together."

Without waiting for an answer, she walks toward the poplar.

"Everything can be easy," the river sings, "easy, easy."

I sit down and clamp my hands over my ears as hard as I can.

Melita walks past a small group of people and takes out her spade. But then she swivels around hard, staring at something.

What is it?

She drops the spade and throws her arms open wide. I can see her mouth opening as she calls to someone. Then she's running and clasping one of the dripping figures. The object of her embrace, a short older woman, just stands there.

Melita takes a step back, a confused look on her face. She's yelling something. She's shaking the woman back and forth.

I leap up and start running over as other shades pull Melita away from her sweetly bemused victim.

Tears sheen down Melita's face. "How could you?" she's yelling, the other shades holding her back. "How could you leave her?"

The woman is oddly, eternally smiling. She turns back to the riverbank as if Melita weren't even there, and sits, dangling her feet in the water. Bliss radiates from her face.

"Mama!" shouts Melita. "Where is she? Where's Philomena?"

I peel her out of the strangers' hands and wrap my arms around her. "Melita, come on. We've got to get away from here."

I steer her up the path from the river, shoving to keep her moving. The sight of her mother terrified me. She was so happy, so empty. So gone.

"There's no point staying here," I say, talking loudly to drown out that insidious song. "Your mother can't tell us anything now. Let's go back to the garden. We'll talk there."

"Persephone, don't you see?" She clutches my arm. "If my mother's here, who's with Philomena?"

I try to make my voice soothing. "Your husband may be home."

"What if he's shipwrecked? What about the flood?"

"Then neighbors will take her in. She'll be all right, Melita."

"Neighbors! Why should they care? It's my neighbors who left their newborn daughter on the hillside." She stops walking. Her voice hardens. "I have to go back. Everything's different now. My daughter needs me."

She stares along the path, her eyes stopping where it disappears into the trees. "I can cross back over the way I came. I'll wait until the ferryman isn't there. The water didn't look very deep."

"There's Cerberus, remember? If you saw his teeth, you'd know! You can't cross the Styx. No one can."

She isn't listening. I reach up and shake her shoulders.

"Don't even think about it," I say. "You'd die."

"I'm already dead."

"But not like that!"

"Look," she says. "People might help when times are good, when everything's easy. But in times like this, only a mother will do whatever it takes to rescue her child."

She plucks my hands off her shoulders. "My mother's gone. My husband's gone. I'm the only one who can save Philomena now."

My ears are ringing.

Only a mother will do whatever it takes to rescue her child.

I hear Melita's words over and over, but I don't see her anymore. I see my mother.

Is that what she's trying to do? Rescue me?

I worry the idea around like a toothless dog trying to grasp a bone.

Impossible! She's trying to punish me. Anyone can see I don't need rescuing. What does she think I am, a kidnap victim?

You didn't leave a note. How was she supposed to know?

But it was obvious I wanted to leave the vale! And someone must have told her I'm fine. No, she wants to be my jailor!

Your savior.

She doesn't care what I want!

She doesn't know why you came.

This is about power!

It's about love.

Suddenly time spirals back to the night before I left. I see my mother's palm pressed to my forehead, and her eager expression, like a traveler on a doorstep hoping to be let in. And back: now her hands are on mine at the loom, her body steadies my small body from behind as I reach from my stool to the high threads. And back: until her hand is reaching far down to mine as we stand in a field of rich earth, the vibration of her song rising in me like water pulled up a stem.

And again I hear Melita's words: *Only a mother will do whatever it takes to rescue her child.*

The voices in my head whip around like a tornado, whirling the good and the bad together so fast, all I see is the blur, and all I feel is the wind.

I open my eyes.

No one. Grass. Weeds. Collecting bag. Trowel lying on the earth.

How long was I gone? I swivel back toward the Lethe, scanning back and forth, panic rising in my throat.

"Melita?"

I don't see her by the riverbank or up ahead on the path to the garden—

But on the road toward the Styx, a small figure is running, arms pumping.

"Melita!"

She's almost up to the trees, and past the trees lies the
bend of that dark river, and Cerberus pacing the banks, his
teeth like swords, sharp enough to slash through bone.

I don't have any choice. I run.

My Voice

How long has she been past that last curve into the trees? I'm running so hard, my lungs are on fire.

"Melita!"

The only sounds I hear in return are the slap of my feet, the clatter of spewing pebbles, my ragged breath.

But as I round the bend, there's a terrible new sound: a growling so deep, it's like the bottom of the ocean, a snarl from three throats joined in a fearsome chord.

I shudder to a stop. There's Melita, up to her thighs in the dark, eddying Styx. It swirls her chiton around her legs, trying to tug her under. And on the close shore stands Cerberus, but Cerberus as I've never seen him. He's like a huge arrow drawn taut in the bow, about to be released toward its target. Six eyes flicker bits of flame; three heads bare teeth in hypnotic snarls.

Suddenly the invisible string twangs and Cerberus leaps. The raging water parts before him as easy as air. Melita raises her hands, screaming, and Cerberus is splashing and snarling and Melita's cries soar skyward—

And then a third voice splits the air down the middle. A voice of power. A voice of command.

My voice.

"Cerberus! Stop!"

The beast pauses, ears pricked. He turns one head my way. The other two are still growling at Melita, but at least he sees me.

"Come here. *Now*, Cerberus."

He turns reluctantly, clambers out of the Styx, and trots to my side. There's still fire in his eyes, but he forces himself to sit like a well-trained hunting dog, waiting for the words that release him to capture his prey.

I hear his hoarse panting, and the relentless river, and then:

"Who *are* you?" asks Melita.

Her eyes are full moons. Her skin has gone dead white. And she's staring, not at Cerberus, but at me. Me, standing there, my hand on the great beast's head.

"Who are you?" she demands again.

"Persephone," I say softly.

"I don't believe you! You're not a servant or a gardener. Who *are* you?"

I say it again, louder this time. "I'm Persephone."

I didn't think her eyes could get any wider, but they do, the instant the truth hits her.

"You mean you're . . ."

"Yes. I'm *that* Persephone."

I cringe at what might come next. Will she fall to her knees in that surging water?

"I should have told you," I say, almost pleading, as I watch the thoughts racing across her face—the angry eyes that call me a traitor; giving way to the gasp and lowering head that call me a queen—but suddenly her head flies back up in revelation.

"If you're a goddess, *you* can save Philomena!" she says eagerly. "Fly across! Make sure she's safe!"

I sigh, a gust of wind. "I can't go back, either."

"Of course you can! You're a goddess. You're queen of the underworld. You can do anything you want."

"I'll try to send a message—"

"A message! Philomena will be dead by the time you do that. She'll never grow up or know love or have children. There's no time for a message."

As she speaks, her face hardens with a new realization. "You don't care, do you?" she says. "I thought we were friends, but it was just a big game to you. You, complaining gods don't respect mortals, and all the time you were tricking me!"

"I was scared I'd lose you!"

Her words are icicle-sharp. "Demeter is your mother! You could have gone back anytime you wanted and made her stop. Then *my* mother would still be alive. *My* daughter would be safe. But you never did a thing. No, you were just pretending to care."

Cerberus growls and I tighten my grip on the center collar, trying to find words to explain.

"If you were ever my friend," Melita says, "if it wasn't all a lie, go to Earth and save my child."

"Melita, I can't!" I cry. "I can't cross the Styx! I can't talk to my mother! I can't do anything!"

"*Can't*," she says bitterly. "That's all you ever say. Can't even try. But it looks like there is one thing you can do." She stares at my hand on the collar. "Hold him so I can cross."

Cerberus feels the desperation building in me. He tugs, whining.

Melita turns against the furious water. "Me, I don't have time for *can't*. Show me now there was friendship between us. Hold that beast back so I can save my child."

Once she takes a step, Cerberus can't restrain himself any longer. With an earsplitting bark he bursts from my grip and into the river.

"Melita," I shout, "stop!"

Cerberus lunges at her, grabbing a mouthful of floating chiton. He shakes the fabric from his teeth—a flash of white rushing downstream. She keeps struggling forward. He leaps again and this time he rakes her arm. Blood oozes up in bright red lines and starts to flow toward the roiling water. He's readying himself for the next attack and still she isn't stopping, and the blood is swirling downstream, weaving into the dark strands of the water, and I open my mouth and scream so loud the air shakes.

"I'll do it!"

Melita stops and turns to me. Cerberus, fangs bared, holds still.

"I'll get Philomena," I say. "I'll make sure she's safe. I don't know how, but I'll do it. Just come back, please."

"Promise," she says.

"I promise."

"Make it a vow that can't be broken."

"I make this sacred vow. I'll return to Earth and find Philomena. I'll make sure she's safe."

A Single Red Drop

"Then run!" says Melita. "*Run!*"

I look at her shivering in the middle of the river, blood dripping down her side. I wade in and wrap my arm around her waist, help her to shore. Tear off a scrap from the bottom of her ripped chiton to bind her arm.

"First I'm getting help for you," I say. "Back in the palace. Come on."

She stands straighter to show me how strong she is. "You'll go faster without me," she says. "I'll be fine, but Philomena—without my mother—no, hurry! Go!"

I look at Cerberus, pacing now on the far bank. Then I stare back the way I came. "And you won't . . ."

She shakes her head. "The Lethe? How could I when I don't know she's safe? Now go!"

I hug her close, letting go reluctantly. And then I run.

The riverbank tries to hold me back, grabbing at me with reeds and branches, snagging my clothes; but soon I burst through the trees into the open. My feet pound along the path faster now, and then the sound is swallowed by long grass, the Lethe's grass, and the river is flowing beside me, filling the air with its seductive song.

Hades won't help you, it sings. *It's all because of you . . . all that death because of you. . . .*

And the song grows louder and louder, until it's ablaze in the air, promising me how good it will feel to lose it all. Everything: Melita's blood swirling into the Styx, and Hades' greed for death before its time, and shades crowding the throne room because of words I didn't speak. The Lethe will wash it all away forever. . . .

I clamp my hands over my ears. And I run.

Silky grass turns to dusty trail, to garden paths laced with thyme. My breath comes in great, ragged shreds. I slow to a walk, clutching my sides. But slowing lets thoughts come into my head, as painful as the Lethe's tune was sweet.

What if Hades won't let me go, what then? He's relishing his growing realm, and he thinks this is just another struggle for power. He doesn't realize my mother is frantic with worry. And the promise I just made—how can he understand that when he doesn't know Melita? He doesn't even know I have a friend! I never mentioned her name to him, not once. And now I know why.

I didn't want to admit I was deceiving her. Deceiving myself.

The thought hurts so much, I stop and close my eyes. I used to think not telling the whole truth was different from a lie. Now I'm not so sure.

But there's no time for this! I gulp in a deep breath, open my eyes—

And there it is. The pomegranate. Lying on the ground where Melita left it, shocking and red and real.

Something makes me lean over and pick it up. It's so heavy, as if a whole world is crowding inside that leathery shell. I run my thumb across the dents and dots and brown patches mottling its skin. All of this came from the glistening seed I planted, a single red drop, as powerful as a word.

I'm about to put the pomegranate back down when suddenly I feel strength surging up my arms, as if whatever's inside this warm, bumpy rind is speaking to my blood. I'm going to need all the strength I can get to convince Hades to let me go, convince him to care. So I grasp it tighter and start striding toward the palace doors, and my husband, and if the fates are willing, Earth.

The Door

I cross the forecourt and climb the steps. This time it's easy finding Hades. Loud voices rise from a closed room. We have company.

That's not going to stop me.

I push open the heavy door, and Hades' voice snaps off abruptly, like a sword coming down on an enemy's neck. There's dead silence. The air is thick. It's like I'm wading into the room.

Hermes stands by the window, his arms crossed tightly in front of his chest. He stares over at me, his mouth a thin, determined slash.

Hades is leaning over our inlaid gaming table, clenching

the sides so tightly, a crack snakes across the polished wood. His eyes blaze at Hermes as pure and destructive as fire, like Cerberus on the attack. His head pivots toward me, and he straightens, letting the table go. Two halves clatter to the floor.

He strides over and slams a possessive arm around my shoulders. I tighten my hold on the pomegranate.

I'm not even going to ask. Whatever it is, I don't care. Nothing will change my mind. I'm going to talk to Hades. Now.

"Hermes, I need to speak with my husband."

Hermes doesn't budge. Hades is gripping me too tightly. I look from one face to the other.

"Alone," I say.

"There isn't time," says Hermes. "I have my orders."

"Damn your orders," says Hades.

He swivels me around to face him. My hand, cradling the pomegranate, is trapped between us.

"Your mother has played her hand," he says, anger dripping like venom.

"She made a deal with Zeus," says Hermes, not moving from the window. "You come back, she stops. No more destruction. She'll allow sun and rain in balance. Crops will grow, animals fatten, people thrive, and the gods will be appeased with their sacrifices again."

"Zeus can do that? He can call me back?" I ask.

The two of them answer simultaneously.

"Yes," says Hermes.

"No," says my husband.

The "no" slides off my back like water. I can't believe my luck! Now I can do everything I need to do, with an easy chariot ride back to Philomena and my mother.

"Give me an hour to change," I say, looking down at my chiton. Mud and dirt mingle with browning smears of blood from Melita's arm.

"What?" says Hades, incredulous. "You want to leave?"

"This won't take long," I say. "There's something I have to do on Earth—I'll tell you later, when there's time—and my mother needs to see I'm all right. She's worried about me; that's why she's trying to bring me home. Back in the throne room, I was still figuring it out. I tried to tell you."

"Oh, you didn't need to tell him," says Hermes. "He knew, from the day you got here."

I shake my head at him. "He's glad to have more subjects, I know that, but he wouldn't keep something this important from me."

But that's no expression of innocence I'm seeing on Hades' brow. He's seething.

"Traitor!" he snarls at Hermes.

Hermes is cold and determined. "He knew your mother was doing everything she could to bring you back, and he liked the results. He said not to tell you."

"Not to tell me!" I stare up into Hades' eyes. "Say that's not true. Go on, say it."

He looks away.

My heart plummets. So he knew all along. That whole time I was worrying about my mother trying to force me back, it was Hades manipulating me, using me to gain power and covering it up with kisses. And I just trotted alongside as obediently as one of his horses.

I'm not feeling so obedient now.

"Mortals have been dying in my name and you didn't bother to tell me? I thought you loved me! But you don't even trust me with the truth. What kind of love is that? Or maybe"—I pause for a second, my disbelief deepening into anger—"maybe you only pretended to love me back in the vale, so I'd come with you! You *knew* what my mother would do to get me back. You *knew* more people would die. Is that all I am for you? A weapon for your war?"

"That's one accusation you can't make," growls Hades. "I didn't pretend. I love you. But I thought once you heard, you'd go soft-hearted and leave. Was I so wrong? Look at you now, ready to run home to your mother."

I don't believe this!

"You never even let me talk about Earth!" I say. "Every time I said the word you cut me off, so you wouldn't lose a single corpse."

The pomegranate is growing heavier in my hand. It must

be packed full of seeds, each one a chance to start the cycle of life again. *That's* what he doesn't understand.

"Don't you remember what you said to me back in the vale?" I ask. "You said we made a cycle complete. Remember?"

"Of course I remember."

"Well, you can't have shades without mortals." My voice grows stronger with each word. "If nobody is born, nobody dies. Who's going to come to the underworld then? No one, not one single shade for the rest of eternity! What kind of cycle is that? And you, the eternal ruler of a static realm, what will you do then—run shades through the Lethe over and over so you can pretend they're new? No, the only way to keep your precious power is to save mankind!"

Hades is speechless after my tirade. When I glance at Hermes I see his mouth is agape.

"So I'm going to Earth," I say. "For the sake of mortals and the sake of our realm. And when I come back, there are going to be some changes around here."

Hermes' mouth snaps shut.

"That's the thing," says Hades. "You won't be coming back."

What? Not come back?

The thought explodes inside me, leaving an echoing hollow in its wake. For the first time, I stare at Hades' eyes, his hands, as if I might never see them again.

"Look," says Hermes in a gentler voice. "I've always been Hades' friend. That's why I didn't tell you before. So I want to make sure you understand everything now. Zeus isn't suggesting you come to Earth for a visit. He's commanding you to live there forever. The underworld is closed to you, as they say, henceforth."

No! They *must* be wrong!

"That's impossible," I insist. "Once my mother sees I'm fine, once I tell her what idiots my husband and I have been, not letting her know"—I stop to look pointedly at Hades—"she'll let me return, and Earth will heal."

"She won't let you return," says Hades in a clipped voice.

"She wants you on Earth," says Hermes.

"She still sees you as a child. But you're a woman, a queen."

Their voices are turning into a chorus, the hard, short lines banging down like nails into a coffin.

"You're giving up your home," says Hermes. "Your work."

"You'll never see me again," says Hades.

"And you won't even save mankind. Demeter has found her weapon."

"She'll scorch the land whenever she wants her way."

"You're giving up everything for nothing."

"If you go, you won't come back."

There's a pause.

"Just so we're clear on that," says Hermes.

They're both staring at me, waiting. One for me to go, the other for me to stay.

In the silence, the pomegranate warms my hand. It tells me I know what I have to do. But that doesn't make it easy.

I look into Hades' eyes. "I'll take my chances," I say. "I'm going."

I hold out the ripe, round fruit. "I grew this with my friend, a shade. I promised to rescue her daughter. To save her, and Earth, I have to go. Even if Zeus didn't command it, I'd go."

Hades stares at the pomegranate as if seeing it for the first time, his eyes opening wide.

"Maybe you're right and this will cost me everything," I say. "Maybe I won't be able to come back here. But then at least you'll know what it's like for mortals, losing what they love."

Losing it forever.

My voice rises and I brandish the red orb in front of his face. "Maybe then you'll think about balance for a change! Yes, I'm going. Don't you see? That's why you'll still have a realm to rule."

Hades listens, thinking.

I don't know whether to shout or cry.

"You've been a glutton for power!" I say. "You kept the

truth from me! You've been thoughtless and selfish and—"

My hand, with its burden, comes to rest on his chest.

"And I love you. I still love you."

I love him so deep down it shakes me, and being angry doesn't change that one bit.

Suddenly, Hades tenses. His eyes dart to the window where Hermes leans, adjusting the wings on his sandals.

"All right. So you're going," says Hades.

Hermes and I both stare in disbelief. Hades is giving in.

"Hermes," he says. "Before this day we were friends. In the name of that friendship, give me a last few moments alone with my wife."

Hermes realizes he's won, and his face relaxes.

"Zeus said not to let Persephone out of my sight." He shifts from foot to foot. "This isn't easy for me, either, you know. Still . . ." He runs his fingers through his hair, thinking. "I guess it's enough if we're in the same room."

He turns his back to us and stares resolutely out the window. "This is the best I can do for your private farewell," he says, and starts humming loudly to create a few moments of privacy.

Hades looks back at me, eager. For a last kiss? He leans in so close our mouths almost touch. Then he says softly, his breath warm in my ear, "Let's share it, then. Your pomegranate."

"Now?"

"Now. As a token of the love that will bind us, even when you're on Earth."

So hushed, so intimate. My anger fades. The only thing I feel is what I risk losing.

I start tugging at the little red crown and one of the spikes breaks off in my hand, a miniature cat's ear. An acrid smell rises, green fresh and red sweet at the same time. The next spike comes off and a fragment of rind. Soon the whole crown is gone, but all I've done is reveal a jagged patch of yellowish pith. I still can't open the fruit.

Maybe it wasn't ready after all. Maybe it fell off too soon.

I pull off another chunk and another, and now all my easy fingerholds are gone. Still the fruit sits there, encased, secretive. Only one tantalizing, shiny spot peers up at me from the pith, a little dark eye.

Hades' breath has been coming faster and faster. Exasperated, he rips the pomegranate from my hand, pulls a knife from his waistband, and slashes into the thick hide.

Red juice splatters my chiton, next to the mud stains and the smears from Melita's bleeding arm. A sharp scent slices the air. A handful of seeds splashes onto the marble floor like drops of blood, an offering.

And they're crowded in—a family of seeds, a womb crammed so tight, the bodies push curved indentations into the hard pulp like a river carves canyons into rock. Each seed barely restrains its load of red juice under a translucent membrane. Through the juice, in the center of each, shines a white core. New life.

Now that the hide is broken, Hades peels a chunk of seeds away; they cling to each other and to their raft of rind. Each seed is faceted like a crystal, and facet fits into facet with the perfect order of a honeycomb.

I tumble a bunch of seeds into my palm. Like beads. Like drops of fire.

Hades takes my wrist, stopping me, the shining drops cradled in my palm.

"If you love me," he whispers, "if you truly want to return to my side, and only then, eat."

I toss them in my mouth.

Sweet and tart, the burst of juice, the crunch of tiny seeds between my teeth. A lingering sharpness on the back of my tongue. Another. And another.

And now I lift my hand to his mouth to complete the ritual.

"Only if you truly love me," I whisper, and he opens his mouth and I feed him.

Now, when I'm on the verge of leaving, now I know. Yes, he wanted my power, whatever he thought it might be. But that wasn't all. He loves me. And now that may have to be enough for eternity.

Hermes clears his throat, turns, and walks toward us.

I can tell Hades is ready to let me go. It's the oddest thing: he looks strong and determined, not defeated at all. That must be what comes with practice ruling a great land. I guess I can carry that much away with me, too.

So I throw my shoulders back, lift my head, and say with as much strength as I can muster, "I'm ready."

"Not quite," says Hades.

He wraps me in his arms and we kiss, a huge kiss, a hungry kiss, a soft kiss, a kiss to last forever.

Until it ends, and I walk, past spatters of blood-red juice, toward the door.

PART THREE
Above Again

Soil, blood, seed—
Let me draw strength from you.
Let it be enough.

The Journey Back

Hermes grips the reins, his eyes glued to the horizon. Below us, the ocean rolls, endless, inexorable. Waves and wind and the mew of a gull are the only sounds. The gull arcs up below the chariot and tilts sideways to peer at me with an inquiring eye. Her curiosity satisfied, she zooms back down. Her wings shift the air.

A thin white ribbon of land begins to unfurl at the ocean's edge. My breath catches, fear and hope mingling together. I've looked down on that land from a chariot exactly once before—down on green hills speckled with sheep, and lakes shining like jewels in the sun, and towns of white houses clustered together like chattering girls. And this time? What will I see?

The white ribbon broadens into a swathe of sand rimming a cove. It's scattered with bright dots like brilliantly colored beetles. But as we come closer, the beetles grow and grow, until suddenly they become broken fishing boats. A tiny figure tugs a dinghy like an ant pulling an oversized leaf. Around him, painted boards lie splintered on the sand.

Beyond the beach, everything is brown and gray under the leaden sky. At first I think this is a rocky area, but then I see twigs strewn across the ground—no, not twigs, tree trunks. Thin lines twist through mud, so many letters etched in clay; they turn into battered stone walls. That's where fields and houses used to stand. There's no green anywhere, not a leaf, or a bud, or a shoot.

Even when the shades in the throne room spoke of crops withering away, of rain stripping the land, even when I saw how many newcomers crowded the floor, I never thought it would be like this: the earth's insides churned up and strewn around like bodies after a grisly battle.

A battle fought in my name.

My hands open and close—I need my spade so I can work that soil! I need plows and hoes and rakes! I need to be a hundred bodies, a thousand, with enough hands to reach into that earth and urge it back toward life.

We fly over a hut that somehow survived intact. A small figure appears at the door, tossing out a bucket of mud. Another flap of the horses' wings and I see someone tugging on a rope, trying to clear away a bloated animal carcass. I feel my stomach rising in my throat.

She was trying to rescue me, I tell myself. *She did this in the name of love.*

But how can I make the leap from that word, *love*, to the carnage spread out below me? My mother cared about rescuing one life: mine. To save me she was willing to starve and suffocate and bury mankind.

How did anyone survive?

The thought fills me with a sense of urgency. Melita was right! A young child alone, what hope would she have down there? How much time do I have to reach her? Am I already too late?

I stare at the earth below, searching for the rock like a rooster's comb, the one Melita said towers over her house. Maybe I can land and find Philomena before we even reach Mount Olympus.

"Go faster," I say.

Hermes shrugs. He must think we're going fast enough. And he's not that good with the horses, anyway, not like Hades.

I've seen them do better. I grab the reins out of Hermes' hands and bring them down with a slap on the horses' backs, urging them on. The air starts whipping by; the ground blurs.

"What do you think you're doing?" shouts Hermes,

snatching back the reins. The chariot jolts sideways, throwing me against the railing.

"Don't you see?" I shout back. "There's no time! Look down there!"

"You forget," he says in a calmer voice. "I've been here every day. That"—he nods down at a man slogging through the mud—"is an improvement."

If Hermes and Hades are right, if I never return to my husband's side, maybe it's what I deserve. Me, the girl who couldn't bother to leave her mother a note: "Ran away with the man I love. All is well. Don't worry."

But wait. Is it *all* my fault? What about Hades? How could he revel in this? And my mother . . .

Guilt, anger, and hope are shoving around inside me like a herd of hungry goats, each demanding a turn.

"Anyway, we're almost there," says Hermes.

The land is rising higher and higher to meet us. Craggy rock faces jut into the clouds, and on one of the uppermost peaks, a gold-pillared temple flashes through sunless skies. Mount Olympus, home of the gods.

The Reunion

A crowd of mortals has gathered. They make room for the chariot to touch down and then jostle around us, so curious and excited, they don't even lower their eyes. A white-bearded man picks up a lyre, and staring sightlessly in my direction, sings out, "Hail, hail Persephone! Persephone is home!"

The crowd takes up the words like eager children repeating a lesson. "Persephone is home! Persephone is home!"

The horses fold their wings and Hermes steps out of the chariot before turning and offering me his hand. The crowd parts and Hermes leads the way up six wide steps onto a porch with a double row of pillars. We pass from glaring sunshine into sudden coolness. The antechamber is empty, a dim rectangle in front of towering wooden doors. Our footsteps echo as Hermes strides up and bangs three times with his staff. The doors swing open and we enter.

There, beneath the gilt-covered ceiling, on a massive throne, sits Zeus. He's majestic, with waves of golden hair falling to his shoulders, a neatly trimmed golden beard, and interest flickering in eyes as blue as a summer sky. His chiton hangs in perfect pleats of soft-spun gold. Next to the throne, a pile of thunderbolts sits within easy reach. And to his left—

But this woman doesn't look like my mother! A faded, night-blue cloak covers her frame, and her shoulders are bowed, like a farmer's wife carrying a load of firewood. For a moment she stares as I approach, her eyes raking my hair, my face, my bare feet, my disheveled dress—and then she strides toward me and wraps me in her arms.

I see it in her face; I feel it in her arms. She does love me.

I sink into her embrace, and for one long, beautiful minute, I let her be my strength.

Then: "My child," she says, stroking my back. "My poor, ravished child."

Wait. Ravished?

My body tenses in her arms. I have some explaining to do.

"We're going home," says my mother. "You'll be safe

from him there. I've strengthened the borders. He'll never get back in."

"I wanted to go," I say, but she's holding me so close, my words smother into her chest.

"Of course, dear," she says soothingly, stroking my head, not having heard a word.

She just needs to understand! I shove myself back, trying to speak louder; my words are a shout in the sudden air.

"I *wanted* to go!"

"And now you *have* gone!" she insists. "You've gone from the underworld forever. You'll never have to see Hades again. That's what I'm trying to tell you."

"But—"

"You see?" she says to Zeus. "She's overwrought, exhausted. I'm taking her back to the vale immediately. She needs rest."

She wraps an arm around my shoulders and takes a step toward the door—toward the vale and my narrow bed and the pink cliffs, reinforced even stronger now . . .

But I'm not the victim she thinks she saved! I'm not the girl she used to shush with a lowering brow! I throw off her arm.

"I want to be with Hades," I say. "I'm his wife, his queen."

She hears the words, but she still doesn't listen. She speaks to me softly, as if calming a frantic, fevered child. "If you were his beloved queen, would you be barefoot, your feet scratched and filthy?" she asks. "Would you be wearing— this?" Her fingers lift a fold of my stained, ripped chiton. "No earrings, then, or bracelet, let alone a crown, to show the honor due your rank?" Her hand rests on my shoulder as she sadly shakes her head. "Hades has been playing with your mind. You've learned to parrot his words to ensure your safety. It's time to face facts. You have been not his queen but his captive. Come home now."

Zeus shifts restlessly on his throne. He turns to a side table and fiddles with some fruit on a golden tray.

King of the gods, ruler of earth and sky . . . So how could Hades have crossed the border if Zeus didn't agree? That means he knew I was going, and approved.

"Zeus," I plead, stepping toward the throne. "Please, she'll listen to you!"

He turns back to me, his eyes widening in surprise.

Then my composure slips and the rest of my words pour out in an ungainly rush. "Tell her I can't go to the vale right away, there are things I need to do here, and after that I need to go back to Hades, even if he has been—"

"That's what I've been saying!" says my mother. "You don't—"

I stretch my arms toward Zeus, my voice too loud. "Listen to—"

Suddenly my lips clamp closed. I try to pull them open,

but they're stuck as tight as a locked trunk. Zeus is putting down his raised hand; a few sparks linger in the air.

"That was getting out of control," he says, his hand drifting back to the platter, searching for something to nibble.

I don't believe this! If I could only shout loud enough, *someone* would have to listen to me! But it's no use. I can't open my mouth. And if I can't explain, how will I get back to Hades, and home? How can I find Philomena if I'm trapped behind pink cliffs?

"I left her alone too much," my mother says to Zeus.

Apparently her mouth is working just fine.

"I thought she was safe in the vale," she continues. "But no, she was as vulnerable as a soft, new bud. That day, when I stood in fields far away and heard her scream, my blood ran cold."

Zeus doesn't say anything. He holds up the shriveled remnants of a bunch of grapes and finds a raisin to chew. My mother turns to me.

"I flew home as fast as I could," she says. "I searched the vale from cliff to pond, meadow to orchard, but I was too late. You were gone."

I can't talk. I might as well listen.

"And so I wrapped myself in this dark cloak of mourning," she says. "For nine days and nights I searched the earth for you, never stopping to eat or drink or sleep. Worry filled me like water fills a jug, leaving no room for air."

She takes my hand, wrapping it in both of hers. "Crops began to wither. I didn't see them. Mortals prayed in desperation for my aid. I didn't hear them. Sacrificial fires darkened the sky. I didn't smell them. I had no time. I had to find you."

She sighs deeply. "I finally learned the truth from Helios. I had to block his sun chariot before he'd tell me he'd seen you in the underworld, with Hades."

A shudder racks her body.

"Dark, despicable Hades! So it was he who ripped you, screaming and struggling, from the vale! And now I knew you shivered on a couch by his side, fearing his every embrace, in a land you could not leave. A land I could not enter."

I shake my head hard, opening my eyes as wide as I can, hoping she'll read the truth there. But her story surges on.

"And Zeus approved of your abduction! He urged me to accept this— What was it you called it, Zeus? This 'match with the ruler of a mighty realm.'" Scorn drips from each syllable. "As if I would abandon you to an eternity with that brute merely because of his rank! And so I did the only thing that could bring you home. I withdrew from gods and mankind, vowing no crops would grow until I saw your face again. For an agonizing year, fields withered beneath my anger. Oxen pulled plows over barren, desiccated earth."

Her voice hardens like molten iron setting into a blade. "And what did Zeus do? Nothing! No, worse than nothing.

He sent me gifts and piles of gold, trying to tempt me away from my vow. Cold, inert, lifeless gold! As if metal meant more than the seeds I destroyed to save you!"

She glares at the throne. "Because Zeus would not act, I blackened the sky with thunderclouds and the deluge fell, scouring the very face off the earth. Finally, finally, mortals' cries reached his ears, and he called you home to me."

She stops, breathing heavily. In the sudden silence, I hear a scurrying outside the door. Lyre strings plunk as something brushes against them; then they're stilled again. Someone was listening. A murmur rises in front of the temple, then fades away. All is stillness.

My spirit catches in my chest. Her beloved barley, her precious wheat—she destroyed what I thought she loved most in the world, because, in truth, she loved something more. Me.

All those crowded graves. Because she thought I was in danger.

Because of words I could not speak.

Those words are still trapped inside me, banging like fists on the door of my heart. How can I open my mouth?

I pull my hand out of hers and start pacing. But she isn't finished yet.

"To think Zeus tried to convince me you were fine! Fine? Look at your chiton!"

I pry at my lips with my fingers.

"I know how it is among mortals," she says. "Their daughters are abducted all the time or forced into miserable marriages by fathers who care only for prestige. But not *my* daughter!"

A strident edge sharpens each word. Zeus's hand drifts toward the thunderbolts, as if he thinks he might need one. Oh, *how* am I going to speak?

"*My* daughter will never have to suffer again," she declares. "For *I* have the power to make Zeus listen! *I* have the power to make the entire earth listen!"

And mortals, I wonder, who listens to them?

I stop and close my eyes.

For one precious moment, I believed everything she did was because of love. But now love and power are both shouting their names. I wanted it to be so pure. Nothing is ever pure.

My mother's voice fills the room. "I have the power to speak for my daughter when she can't speak for herself!"

Then a new note enters the fray.

"That's just it," says Hermes from the shadows. "She can't speak. You've sealed her shut."

"Ah, I forgot," says Zeus, waving his hand.

My lips unlock, my mouth opens.

But for a moment, I'm still silent. Because I don't want

to shout, or yell, or whine that she's got it all wrong. I don't want to hide the hard parts away, like I always did before, avoiding her thunderstorms. I'm going to do this right.

I take a deep breath and step toward my mother.

"Yes, your power helped bring me here," I say. My voice is soft and clear. "But I also chose to come back. Because there's something I need to say to you, something I should have said a long time ago. Can you listen to me? Do you have *that* power?"

She glances from my soiled chiton to my determined face, as if trying to reconcile the two. With obvious effort, she nods.

I turn to Zeus. "Please let me speak," I say. "Don't seal my words away."

Looking intrigued, he nods as well.

I look into my mother's eyes. "I chose to come back to Earth, but I also chose my life with Hades. You see, I love him."

She opens her mouth, but I hold up my hand to stop her. She stares at my hand, shocked.

"He found his way into the vale," I say, each word crisp. "He came to find me, and I snuck away to meet him, again and again and again. I had to keep seeing him. He makes me feel alive because he sees me. He believes in me."

Even when he's as obsessed with power as my mother, I know he believes in me.

The color is draining from her face.

"There was no abduction," I say. "Hades asked me if I wanted to come to the underworld with him. He made sure I knew it would be forever. And I went, willingly."

Silence hangs in the air. Then: "You would have told me," she says, so quietly I strain to hear. "You would have told your friends."

I shake my head. "I wasn't strong enough. I thought you'd lock me in my room and I'd never see Hades again. So I lied."

The words are as painful as fire in my throat, in the air.

"And later, I still didn't tell you. I should have written a note or sent word with Hermes. I left it to everyone else to tell you where I'd gone, and then wondered why they didn't act. Instead of doing it myself."

"But your clothes!"

"Don't look at my clothes," I say. "Look at my face."

She stares and stares, and then her cheeks begin to shine. It takes me a moment to realize what I'm witnessing. For the first time in my life, I'm seeing my mother cry.

And then her voice bursts out, an anguished keening. "All for nothing!" She closes her eyes, swaying back and forth. "Destroyed and all for nothing! Oh, my sweet wheat, my beloved barley—what have I done?"

I wrap her in my arms, and my tears mingle with hers.

Yes, I think, what have you done? What have I done?

❧❧

She steps back and looks at me. It's as if the veils she always saw me through, veils woven of words like *child* and *maiden*, are gone; she's seeing me for the first time.

"You love him," she says.

"Yes," I say. "I want to be with him."

"Then you shall."

Sounding once again like a goddess in charge, she turns to the back of the room. "Hermes! Prepare the chariot. Persephone is returning to the underworld."

Zeus has been listening, watching the scene unfold, but now he leans forward, gripping the arms of his throne. "Oh, no she isn't," he snaps. "Listen, Demeter, this has gone on long enough! First Hades bends the rules to marry her, and then you damn near destroy Earth to bring her back here—do you think the border is an open gate she can stroll through a hundred times a day?" His face is turning red. "No, as long as the girl didn't eat or drink in the under-world . . . Did any nectar cross your lips, Persephone?"

Nectar? No, not a sip.

"Any bread?" he continues. "Figs? Eggs? No? Then I'm sorry, Demeter, but she stays on Earth. Look at this!" He flourishes the desiccated bit of vine with its shriveled raisins. "There's nothing decent to eat around here, with all this border-crossing nonsense. You made me bring her back, and I bent all the rules to do it. This is where she stays!"

My mother is drawing in her breath, preparing to blast back at him, when a most incongruous sound rises from the back of the room. Hermes is laughing.

"What's so damn funny?" demands Zeus.

Hermes strolls out of the pillars' shade and into golden light. A grin splashes across his face.

"Very clever," he says. "Oh, Hades is a wily one! You can't help but admire him, can you?"

"Admire that troublemaker?" says Zeus. "Why should I?"

"There I was," says Hermes, "turning my back so the lovebirds could say a private farewell. I only heard a whispered word or two. 'If you love me.' I think that's what Hades said. And 'Let's share it.'" Hermes shakes his head in amusement. "He knew if I saw, my orders would force me to stop him. Because as Zeus has so rightly pointed out, food is the only thing with the power to bind Persephone eternally to the underworld, the only thing capable of overruling the king of the gods himself. I saw the evidence as we left, but I didn't realize what it meant. Until now."

He puts his hands on his hips, his smile as broad as his stance. "Persephone," he says, "why don't you tell them what made those stains on your chiton?"

I look down, running my fingers over fabric smeared with dirt, ripped by clutching branches, brown with dried blood. And all down the front: red red red—stains as shocking and bright as each bursting pomegranate seed.

Suddenly, I see everything—the welcoming banquets, Hades' fingers running along my thigh in the throne room as he offered me bread, the impatient way he slashed the rind with his knife—now I see what it all meant.

"I did eat in the underworld!" I proclaim, joyfully lifting the fabric to display the evidence. "I ate seeds from a pomegranate I grew! I shared it with Hades!"

Hades, so careful to make sure it was what I wanted, too, even if he couldn't spell it out for me with Hermes in the room. I hear his whispered words again; I feel his breath warm in my ear. *If you truly want to return to my side, and only then, eat.*

Knowing food would bring me home to him. Tactician. Ruler. Husband. Love.

I close my eyes, seeing his face, feeling his arms, his broad hands. Hades.

"He didn't have to let you leave, after that," my mother says softly. "He loves you enough to let you go. And that's what I need to do, too."

"Damn it all," says Zeus, stamping his immortal foot. "Back and forth, back and forth, like a bunch of love letters. All right then, Persephone returns to the underworld. But I'm telling you, this is absolutely the last time, and only because of the pomegranate. Don't think you'll get anywhere by changing your mind again, Demeter. She's going back for good, regardless of what you want."

"But this *is* what I want," says my mother, looking at me, her voice surprisingly gentle. "Because it's what Persephone wants. And it seems she's capable of making her own choices."

I smile, grasping her hand. But then I see her eyes staring at me, and I realize she's trying to soak up as much of me as she can, enough to last her . . . forever.

"Off you go, then," says Zeus. "Immediately."

I think of how rich the earth used to be and could be again. Groves crowded with fat, ripe olives. The way black soil smells when it's been turned. I think of my mother trying to save me and Melita risking the fangs of Cerberus for her daughter.

And then I remember.

"I can't go right away!"

They both turn to me sharply, heads cocked sideways like birds.

"Before I go, I need some time on Earth." I stride toward Zeus and grab the brittle grapevine from his platter. "This is what I've got to fix! I need to get my hands in the soil and help make it bloom again. And there's something else. In the underworld, I was friends with a mortal, and I made her a promise."

"A promise to a mortal? Never a good idea," says Zeus.

"Let her speak," says my mother.

"I promised I'd find her daughter and make sure she's safe. If I go back now, I can't keep my word."

"Promises must be kept," says my mother.

"No," says Zeus, pointing his finger at me. "You need to leave this minute. You shouldn't even be here. Someone else can help the mortal child."

"I promised to do this myself!"

He shakes his head. Light glances off his hair like golden feathers. Eagle feathers. He's parting his lips to speak again when an idea flies into my head, fully formed.

"Zeus—"

"Don't argue," he says. "There are rules to be followed."

But I keep going. "The rule says food is binding. But there are different ways to bind. A bird leaves its home when frost falls. It spends the winter in a distant land. But come spring, the bird returns to its first home."

"So?" says Zeus.

"Don't you see? The bird is bound to depart each year but not to stay away. It always comes back again to its first home. I can be bound to the underworld and still return to Earth each year."

A smile warms my mother's face.

"I have a home in the underworld, and a husband, and work I'm learning to do. But if I stay there forever, my mother will keep grieving. I don't think a grief-stricken goddess will create abundant harvests, do you?"

Zeus is looking thoughtful.

"I'll fulfill my promise, and maybe . . ." I look at my mother. "Maybe I could work for a while by my mother's side. I did a lot of gardening in the underworld. Some people think I have a knack for it."

As I speak, I lift my hand, and Zeus's mouth drops open. A gasp escapes from my mother's lips. I follow their eyes.

From the shriveled bit of grapevine, tiny green leaves are springing. There, amidst the brown remnants, are two ripe grapes, a juicy, intoxicating purple.

Hades was right. He saw it all along. I do have power.

"Here's what I want," I say to Zeus. "To stay here part of each year and then spend the rest in the underworld, ruling by my husband's side. Every year I'll return to Earth. That should fulfill the requirements."

"Hmm," says Zeus, still eyeing the grapes. "Very clever. I like it."

"As do I," says my mother.

"So be it," says Zeus, his voice booming. "Persephone's sojourn on Earth will begin now, to help the land heal. Hermes, perhaps you'd like to let Hades know."

Hermes grins at me. "This should put me back on good terms with the old rascal," he says.

"Stop talking!" I say. "Go! Tell him!"

Fly like the wind to my husband and tell him he'll hold me again.

"I'm going, I'm going," says Hermes. "I'll be back for you in a few months. Maybe next time we'll have a smoother ride!"

He wheels around and out the door. In a moment there's a roar from the crowd as the black horses rise, pulling a chariot as light as air.

Immortalized

And now I need to find Philomena.

My mother and I walk side by side out the doors and into the shadowy anteroom. Beyond the pillars, a huge crowd stands in the blazing sun, staring up at a tiny dot disappearing into the sky.

I start to walk forward, but my mother puts her hand on my arm. "Give them just a moment," she whispers. "They'll move on."

The blind bard plucks out a few bold notes on his lyre, and everyone gathers around him expectantly. Has he already immortalized today's events in a song? Now the crowd stills, and the white-bearded bard begins to sing, his voice deep and confident.

"Hideous Hades ripped her away
From her mother's arms that fateful day,
When all she wanted to do was stay
Safe in her mother's arms, oh!"

He nods at the crowd expectantly and they echo the last
line back: "Safe in her mother's arms, oh!"

Wait! That's all wrong! My mother's hand tenses, and she
glances at me.

"Down to the sulfurous lands below
He forced the cowering maid to go,
Not heeding her tears, their endless flow—
He only saw her charms, oh!"

"He only saw her charms, oh!" roars the crowd in
unison.

"Demeter, the goddess of grain and good
Reacted as any mother would:
Denied her daughter, she sent a flood
Over the valleys and farms, oh!"

"Over the valleys and farms, oh!"

"Till Zeus, he heard the clamorous cry
And said, 'Then bring Persephone nigh!'
And back with the maiden did Hermes fly,
Answering all the alarms, oh!"

"Answering all the alarms, oh!"

"Sweet girl-child, no longer chafe,
In Hades' arms, his captive waif.
Demeter's strength will keep you safe,
Safe in your mother's arms, oh!"

"Safe in your mother's arms, oh!" the crowd sings one last time, before bursting out in a thunderous round of applause.

My mother's eyes narrow. "The mortals are mistaken," she says. "I'll tell them the truth."

This time I'm the one pulling her back into the anteroom. "Wait."

She stops. There's a long pause while I gather my words.

"These people have been through drought and famine and flood," I finally say. "They've lost crops and homes, buried those they love. With this song, people are saying they suffered for a reason: so you could save me. But if they're told it was for nothing, because I couldn't speak my mind . . ."

I hear her breath.

"Mortals need something to believe in so they can get back behind their plows," I say. "If this is the story they need, shouldn't we let them have it?"

The darkness in here makes her eyes look like bottomless pools.

After the bard has been raised onto men's shoulders, after he's strummed and sung the crowd downhill, my mother turns to me. She takes a step, I take a step, and then our arms are wrapped so tightly around each other, there's no space between us.

Philomena

"I'll come with you," says my mother.

I shake my head. I have to do this on my own.

I've told her about Melita and Philomena and my only clues: a mountain valley, a river and goats, and a crag with five points like a rooster's comb. Now my mother closes her eyes, thinking so deep it looks like she's summoning information up from the earth. Her eyes snap open.

"Yes," she says, "I saw it, when I wandered the land searching for you."

She points to a haze of mountains rising in the distance. She asks if I want a chariot, a horse, but I have a feeling I need to go on foot, even though it will take longer.

She takes the dark-blue cloak from her shoulders and wraps me in it to keep the brisk spring breeze at bay.

"When the time comes to act, look inside yourself," she says. "You'll find what you need."

Her hands lift reluctantly from my shoulders and she watches me stride away, leaving the temple far behind.

Fields, valleys, and now mountain paths—everywhere I go, mortals are working from dawn to dusk, fighting to reclaim the land. Their strength amazes me. And everywhere I go, the earth begins to shimmer with a faint, incandescent green as the first hints of growth take hold.

Let it mean Philomena is safe. Let me be in time.

Now, climbing up a valley by the side of a lively stream, I see the crag with five points: Melita's cockscomb rock. My heart catches. The mountainside is dotted with small farms where women are scrubbing, men are rebuilding, and children are clearing away rocks and sticks. How will I know which of these farms is the right one?

I see a woman vigorously spading a patch of ground just the right size for a vegetable garden. Hiding my face beneath the cloak's oversized hood, I approach and ask the way to Melita's farm. She straightens, putting a hand on her sore back.

"She's long dead, that one," she says.

"It's her baby I'm looking for."

"Not such a baby anymore, is she? Poor thing." She

sighs, shaking her head. "They say an old widow moved in up there, took it over as her own. In these times, who could stop her? Says she owns it all, I hear: the farmhouse, the goat, and the child."

"Owns her?" I ask. "You mean—"

She nods, turning back to her plot of earth. "That's the way of it," she says. "In these times, what can you do?"

I take off at a run on the path she showed me. The trail grows narrower and rougher. I round a bend and now the rooster rock is looming almost directly overhead. There, in a clearing near the banks of the river, stands a small house. Part of the roof has fallen in. A goat, all ribs, rummages in the mud. And in front of the house, a little girl is lugging rocks toward a big pile. They must weigh almost as much as she does.

She lifts her head. I push back my hood a few inches so I can see her better.

The eyes looking back at me are a deep, warm green, like olives hanging on a tree in the sun. The child's hair may be bedraggled, but it's curly and dark. And there, on her shoulder, is a birthmark shaped like a flower with four petals, the mark that made her parents call her their little blossom. It's Philomena.

But how fast human time passes! Melita talked about a toddler on pudgy legs. This child has already been set to work, although she looks young for it and too thin. Her elbows jut out overlarge from bony arms. She's daubed with layers of dirt; she hasn't been bathed in weeks.

"Philomena," I say softly, pushing my hood back all the way so she can see my face. I don't want her to be scared. "Your mother sent me."

She plops her rock back down and starts to walk toward me, as if she knows me. I bend down, opening my arms toward her smile, and she rushes right into my embrace. I wrap her up close and warm, gratitude filling me from head to toe. Gratitude for having found her. For her big, warm eyes. For the way she came into my arms. Gratitude that she's Melita's daughter.

"Get away from that brat!"

An old woman clumps out of the house, anger darkening a face lined with cruelty.

"You ain't takin' her," she says.

I stand up, still holding Philomena. She wraps her arms and legs around me and burrows into me. I can feel her thin body shivering.

"This is Melita's child, not yours," I say.

"You ain't Melita, neither, far as I can tell," rasps the crone. She reaches down for a heavy stick. "I got food invested in this girl. I been keepin' her in line. That means she's mine, same as if I bought her."

I look down at Philomena's skinny arms. They're black and blue and yellow with old bruises.

My head flies back up and my eyes blaze at the woman who did this. "How dare you beat her! How dare you! She needs love, not your brutality!"

The woman barks what's meant to be a laugh. "Love? Who's got time for that? I been feedin' her, and I'm goin' to get the work out of her. She ain't good for much yet, but in a few years she'll earn her keep. Put her down."

She starts walking toward us, holding the stick in both hands. I tighten my arms around Philomena. Anger rumbles up through me. I never felt this determined before.

And now I feel energy surging up from the earth, through my body, until it fills every part of me—blood, bone, skin, breath—and a huge voice roars out of me, more powerful than the voice that stopped Cerberus in his tracks.

"You will not touch this child!"

Her eyes widening in terror, the woman drops the stick. She plunges to her knees in the dirt.

I look down, and down, and down. I'm as tall as a tree. A blinding light surrounds me.

I *am* a goddess.

I marshal the power swirling around me.

"Spare me! Spare me!" shrieks the woman. "I ain't worth your anger!"

"Go," I command, my voice ringing against the valley walls. "Depart and never return. Leave now and that will be your punishment, though you deserve worse. But if you stay . . ."

Without waiting to hear the rest of my sentence, the crone scrambles to her feet and careens helter-skelter down the rocky path. I watch until she's out of sight. Then I look back down at Philomena.

She's not scared. She's snuggling as deep into me as she can, and she's smiling.

I move into the little house with Philomena, and now I'm back to working with my hands again, scrubbing, clearing rocks from the garden patch, turning the soil. Philomena follows me everywhere, helping wherever she can. On a high shelf I find a round of hard cheese that somehow evaded the old woman, and I feed the hungry child as much as she'll eat. Her bruises are starting to heal.

At night I sleep with her softness cradled in my arms. Her breath is like music. I wish Hades could hear it, too. I imagine the three of us lying here together, his arms and mine weaving a nest for a child's night breathing.

On the seventh morning, I jolt awake from a dream that was so vivid, it felt real. I saw a man with Philomena's eyes. He was struggling to get home, but his purse was empty, and a stocky brute was demanding another year's work to pay off a debt.

I disentangle myself from Philomena and leave her slumbering in the bed. Wrapping myself in the dark-blue cloak, I sit by the fire and close my eyes. I go deep, deep inside myself, so far it's like I'm in a different world. I summon up the dream again and put myself in it.

I'm in the room with the two men. The man with Philomena's eyes is slouched forward on his bench, his head buried in his hands. I tiptoe up to him and whisper in his ear, "Say you'll wager your freedom on a game of dice."

He jerks up, staring around the room and trying to find the source of my voice.

"Do this," I say gently. "Say if he wins, you'll work for two years without complaint, but if you win, you go free, all your debts erased. I will help you. Your daughter needs you."

He breathes in deeply, then makes the proposal. The stocky man nods and pulls a handful of dice from his clinking purse. He rolls first. A decent roll.

Then the man with Philomena's eyes picks up the dice, and I wrap them in golden light. When he tosses them on the table I keep each one rolling until the number I want is on top.

The big fellow slams his fist on the table. The man with Philomena's eyes grabs his cloak and runs out the door.

Now Philomena is stirring and the day begins. The house is clean, vegetable shoots poke up eagerly from rich garden soil, and the goat bleats happily around the rocks, nibbling young grasses. Afternoon turns to evening. As the clouds turn pink, a bright whistle rises from down the path. It's him.

I gather Philomena in my arms one more time. I tell her I'll be back again someday. She wriggles down and runs off toward the whistle. And then I'm gone.

Footprints

I tell my mother I'm ready to come with her to the fields. She shifts the basket of grain from one hand to the other, momentarily at a loss for words. Then she gives a little smile and nods.

"Oh, right," she says.

This doesn't come easily for her, sharing.

We arrive alone on a plowed field in the cool morning air. I take off my sandals so the black earth squishes up between my toes. Its energy rises through my feet, up my calves and thighs, into my belly, and through my whole bloodstream. I close my eyes and breathe in the rich, mineral scent. I've missed the feel of this earth, its rhythm and its voice.

And then there's a song rising from the turned earth, and it's in me and through me and all around in the soil that roots me. It's a calling song, calling seeds to sprout and roots to stretch, calling green life to surge up stems and lift leaves to the sun like hands raised in prayer.

I open my eyes and there, at the edge of the field, the black bones of a cherry tree are bursting into flower. How did I miss that before? The petals billow like great puffs of pink smoke. I'm as drugged by their beauty as I was by the scent of narcissus so long ago. I let it pull me across the soil until I can run my finger along a leaf's edge. It's jagged, like a cricket's leg.

I realize now how much I've missed Earth, all of it: this serrate leaf, on this tree; and these grains of soil, moist beneath my feet; and the perfume of blossom and loam and fresh breeze mingling in the air.

A gust of wind wakes me from my reverie, blowing a flock of pink petals from the tree. They swirl down, landing on my hair and shoulders. Laughing, I turn to show them to my mother.

She hasn't budged. She's back where we started, staring at the ground. I follow her eyes.

Each footprint I made in the soil is bursting with green. Those nearest me are just brightening with miniature leaves nestled next to the dirt. But beside my mother, where I first felt the earth's song, the outlines of my heels and toes are blurring beneath eager, thrusting plants, some already a few inches high. If I look steadily enough, I can actually see them growing.

I look up at my mother's face. Now she's staring at me, her eyes as huge and round and blue as the sky. Her hands hang limp and empty at her sides; she's dropped her basket, spilling all the grain out on the ground. In the air around me and under my feet, everything is thrumming.

A bird calls out in single notes, a cascade of three.

The Ring

I'm wandering along by myself today, following where my feet want to go. Earth and I have this agreement: I help her green and bloom, and she fills my ears, nose, eyes, tongue, and fingers with indescribable beauty.

The trail winds up a hillside. Under a sturdy pine, a chorus of daffodils blazes a vibrant yellow song. Rhododendrons line the path, fat buds jostling among shiny green leaves. I reach up to stroke a bud; it starts to uncrumple into a purple flower, still shell-shaped, like a wet chick.

I hear footsteps coming up the trail behind me and I turn.

"Hermes!" I cry in delight.

I run toward him, reaching out to grab his hands.

"How is he?" I ask eagerly. "What did he say? Does he miss me? Is he busy with the horses? How is he doing with the greetings now that I'm not there? What was he wearing when you saw him? Did he—"

"Whoa!" Hermes chuckles, giving my hands a squeeze, then letting go to run his fingers through his curls. "You need to let me talk if you want to know the answers."

I lift my hand to my lips and pretend to turn a key, locking them shut. Hermes collapses in laughter, and now I have to wait a full minute while he regains his composure.

"Oh, that's a good one!" he finally says, snorting. "Not allowed to talk!"

"Hurry up, Hermes. Tell me how he is."

"Impatient for you to come back, that's how he is. Lots of pacing, as if that could make any difference. Some trouble sleeping, he said, without you there."

I sigh in contentment.

"Got himself a new horse to break in," says Hermes. "He thinks that will help take his mind off the waiting. Oh, and he started this system for the shades, some kind of announcement board. When I bring over newcomers now, their names get etched on this big wall. There's always a cluster of shades waiting around to check the new names and there's . . ."

He did it! My idea to let shades know when their loved ones arrive, Hades put it in place!

". . . lots more hugging going on around there. It's kind

of noisy, if you ask me. And you should have heard your friend when I told her you'd found her daughter. Oh, and I almost forgot!"

He reaches into his bag and pulls out a small wooden box tied with a scarlet ribbon. "He said to give this to you. To remember him until you get back, that's what he said."

I grab it out of his hands and start picking at the knot.

"Would I have been in trouble if I'd forgotten that!" says Hermes.

I open the box, and there, nestled in purple cloth, lies a small golden ring. I slip it onto my finger, lifting my hand to see the design. A ripe, round pomegranate is embossed on the shining band.

If you love me, if you truly want to return to my side . . .

A pomegranate, the seeds that will bring us together again and again and again. My heart overflows with joy and longing. Soon. I'll be back soon. . . .

"I'd better be going," says Hermes. "Lots to do, I'm afraid. But I'll see you next—"

"Wait!" I cry. "Can you carry something back for me?"

He nods. I run over to the daffodils and gather a dozen stems. If only they were narcissus! I lay them in Hermes' arms. It's not enough! I snap off some rhododendron branches, now flowering, and add them to the pile, and then some twigs with leaves so new they're translucent, traced with veins like dragonfly wings, and—

"Stop!" cries Hermes, peering over the top of the pile. "It's not like I have the chariot today. Maybe next time you'll think of something smaller to send."

He takes off down the trail and disappears around a bend, leaving me alone again.

I look down at my hand and the golden ring encircling my finger. I press it to my cheek, covering it with my other hand to hold it as close as I can.

Not so alone, after all.

Goddesses

Only six days now and I head home again. Just thinking about Hades makes my heart beat so fast I get dizzy.

So much has happened. Those first light-filled leaves gave way almost overnight to heavy branches and dense shade. Everywhere you look there's green. All that mud coated the ground with new life, even richer than before.

Sometimes I go to orchards or fields with my mother, but more often I go by myself. Just because we realized we love each other doesn't mean it's easy for us to be together all the time. I like to stretch my wings and explore. And my mother— Well, think about it! She's always needed her solitude, roaming her blossoming sanctuary and being one with the green and the growing.

Tomorrow we're going to be worshiped together for the first time at the new temple on top of the hill. *Our* temple.

"Don't forget," she said. "Wear something grand."

I reach out to some blossoms for strength. This is going to be interesting.

A huge crowd stares reverently at the stone altar in front of the columns. I've never seen so many people in one place.

My mother leans over and whispers in my ear. "Now we go into the statues," she says.

Two towering figures stand side by side, brilliantly painted, laden with gold—but underneath, hard, cold, unmoving stone. I stare at the draped folds of my statue's chiton, thinking back to the time I saw a sculptor carving my face from marble. I realize I don't want to enter the statue. I've worked so hard to be more than a figurehead.

"You go ahead," I say. "I'll watch from out here."

"But it's always done this way," she whispers, impatient.

"*You've* always done it this way."

She opens her mouth to snap at me, but then the priestess intones her name, and the crowd takes it up like a chant, and I see my mother's face change. She drinks up the praise as if it's nourishing her. The priestess pours a libation, and my mother nods appreciatively. The mortals, at least, are doing things to her liking.

Staring at me pointedly, my mother steps into her statue. Something shifts subtly in the stone. Her eyes gaze out from its eyes.

The priestess sings of grain and light, dark and death, as if my mother's golden wheat becomes a blazing torch and I help people carry that light with them into the underworld.

And now the priestess pours a second libation, this time intoning *my* name. Chanting after her, everyone turns toward my statue, the empty statue, and bows.

Everyone, that is, except for one old, white-bearded man. His eyes stare sightlessly ahead; a lyre is strung over his shoulder. He sniffs the air, smiling as if inhaling perfume from the freshest spring flowers. Then he turns directly toward me and bows.

The bard. The one who crouched outside the door of Zeus's temple as my mother told her story. The one whose lyre I heard as he rushed from the temple to write his song— too soon, before I set the story straight.

I see the priestess moving her lips at the altar, but I don't hear her. Instead, I'm hearing his song. *Hideous Hades ripped her away* . . .

I know it by heart. Everyone does now. Mothers croon it to their babies. Men sing it as they sip wine together late at night. Shepherds whistle it as they wander with their flocks.

Kidnapped, that's what it says. Forced against my will.

Something in me longs to appear before these people and

tell the real story. Just once! But deep down I know: that song is stronger than the truth.

The priestess reaches into a basket and brings up a pomegranate. Splitting it open, she starts to sing of a beloved girl-child, trapped in a brute's arms and bound by blood-red seeds.

But the seeds aren't really what bind me. No, they're just sweet excuses. I'm returning to the underworld because I need to be with Hades. Once I said his arm would be my true home. And it is. It always will be. The land of death, receiver of so many: I went there so I could live.

The crowd starts to drift away and my mother comes out of her statue. She looks at me with a mixture of exasperation and pride.

"No statue?" she says.

"No statue."

She asks if I'm coming with her to the fields, but I smile and say I need some time by myself. I watch her walking away, so graceful, her palms turning up to soak in the sun. There will be plenty of time to join her next year.

Right now, I only want to think of the underworld and the one who waits for me there. Five more days! How will I live until then?

Home

Olive trees and waving fields become a blur of green below us. I've waited all these months; I can't wait any longer.

"Faster, Hermes," I say. "Faster."

Hermes shrugs, but Abastor hears me and twitches his ears—beautiful Abastor, eager to bring me home—and then his muscular neck is stretching out farther; his wings picking up their pace. The other horses immediately follow suit. Wind sings past my cheeks, strokes my bare arms.

Hermes' knuckles tighten around the reins. He throws me a look, but a quick one; the surging horses take all his attention.

Now rocky land, now beach, now ocean spreading out

below, blue beneath the bright blue sky. Near shore, boats ply the waves, but soon we're beyond where even the bravest mortals go. There's nothing now but endless blue, ocean and sky merging into one seamless whole. I strain my eyes over the infinite sameness, searching.

Then suddenly, there it is: a thin line splitting the universe in two.

We fly lower and the line thickens, takes on the weight and form of land. That's the Styx below us now, and Charon, a tiny figure in a sailor's cap, waving up from its banks.

I've almost stopped breathing. Where is Hades? In the palace? The stables? And then I see him, pacing by the oak tree on the hill below my garden, his purple cloak whipping with each turn—

"There!" I cry, but I didn't need to say anything; Abastor already knows, and we're slowing, circling, landing in a flap of wings and clatter of hooves.

Hades strides toward the chariot, but I can't wait. I leap out, into his arms, and home.

Author's Note

Like many before me, I've taken the bones of a myth and made it my own. The story Demeter tells in front of Zeus's throne, the story the bard overhears and spreads to mankind, is based on a Greek myth often called "The Rape of Persephone."

Persephone, it says, was picking flowers in the Vale of Enna when a fragrant narcissus tempted her close. The moment she snapped the flower's stem, the earth split open. Hades appeared and carried her off, screaming and struggling. When Demeter learned her daughter was trapped in the underworld, she withdrew from gods and mankind, vowing that no crops would grow until she saw Persephone again. Famine devastated the earth. Finally, Zeus commanded Hermes to bring the girl home. But Hades had already fed her pomegranate seeds, binding her to his side forever. Each winter, when she lives below, the earth shivers and nothing grows. Each spring she returns to her mother, and the earth bursts into bloom.

What would it look like, I wondered, if Persephone wasn't carried back and forth against her will but made her own choices?

I used research for inspiration rather than historical exactitude, drawing details from across hundreds of years and miles and using them as jumping-off places. The real Thesmophoria referred to Persephone's abduction, but in the sixth chapter I have the festival preceding her departure from the vale. And while the Styx and Lethe come from Greek myth, the land I've placed them in is my own creation. The Greeks themselves were opportunists when it came to depicting the underworld in art and poetry. I've followed their lead in using whatever served my story.

Myths are retold for thousands of years because they speak to something deep in our hearts. This is what the myth of Persephone said to mine.

Thank You

So many people have walked with me on this journey. For insightful readings, inspiration, and endless encouragement, I especially want to thank Elisabeth Benfey, Eileen Pettycrew, Susan Blackaby, Linda Zuckerman, and Kelly Lenox—this book would not exist without you. I am lucky to have such a remarkable and supportive family: my parents, Warren and Gerda Rovetch, and my sisters, Lissa Rovetch and Jennifer Rovetch. Thank you to the amazing Greenwillow team; to Steve Geck, my editor, for understanding Persephone from the start and leading this book deeper; and to Nancy Gallt, my agent, for helping it fledge into the world. And thank you, thank you, thank you, Richard, Sam, and Kate.